**Ode To Broken Things**

# Ode To Broken Things
*A Novel*

Dipika Mukherjee

# Published by Repeater Books

An imprint of Watkins Media Ltd

19-21 Cecil Court
London
WC2N 4EZ
UK
www.repeaterbooks.com
A Repeater Books paperback original 2016
1

Distributed in the United States by Random House, Inc., New York.

Cover design: Johnny Bull
Typography and typesetting: Jan Middendorp
Typefaces: Chaparral Pro and Stevie Sans

ISBN: 978-1-910924-14-3
Ebook ISBN: 978-1-910924-15-0

May whatever breaks
be reconstructed by the sea
with the long labor of its tides.
So many useless things
which nobody broke
but which got broken anyway.

Pablo Neruda

*Dedicated to the memory of my two Didas,*
*Latika Chatterjee & Binapani Sengupta,*
*fabricators of fables and magicians of storytelling...*
*and Delip Kumar Dutt, son of the Malaysian soil.*

*And for the vanquishers of my personal demons...*
*Prasanta, Arohan, Arush*

Dissected to its constituent parts, Malaysia was a hope-less mess of conflicting priorities, mutually unintelligible languages, contradictory cultures and blinkered religions. Malaysia's politics were divisive, its economy exploitative, its pillars of authority buttressed by an impenetrable scaffolding of draconian laws upheld by a parliament in which dominance seemed to matter far more than debate. There was no reason for Malaysia to have survived this far...

But Malaysia had.

Rehman Rashid, *A Malaysian Journey*

It is estimated that between 1900 and 1940 alone, a total of about 16 million Indian and Chinese immigrants landed in Malaya. This century has witnessed only one other movement on this scale – the migration of Europeans to the United States of America totaling some 19 million during the same four decades.

Kernial Singh Sandhu, *Some Preliminary observations of the origins and characteristics of Indian Migration to Malaya*

**Two months earlier**

# Prologue

When his cellphone rang at two in the morning, Colonel S picked it up and, still blurry from sleep, thought, Stupid bitch, she's finally done it. The person on the line spoke slowly. When Colonel S understood what he was being told, he swung his legs over the side of the bed, rushed out, and got into the car, heading for the abandoned construction site in Shah Alam. A band of fear briefly tightened around his heart as he saw the figures in the darkness. *This was it then!* But the figures seemed diminished by the tall *lalang* waving in the slight breeze and he could feel the moist night, satiny with humidity, cloaking him in its susurrations. The clouds erased the moon.

He could see the princeling, an important senior minister in the Malaysian cabinet, flanked by a junior minister. The princeling was tall and looked even more stooped in the moonlight as he struggled to light his cigarette. His wife stood ramrod straight next to him, her hennaed red hair a blurry fuzz under the scarf covering her head.

Colonel S allowed himself a smile. So this was going to be a circus with a prime-time audience. The princeling may have political clout in Malaysia – the royal blood flowing in his wife's veins didn't hurt – but he could be so easily manipulated by friends like the young minister, now standing by his side.

The two bodyguards flanking the princeling swivelled their heads simultaneously; there was the sound of a car approaching. As the princeling's nervous fingers dropped the lit cigarette, the young minister ground it into the wet soil deliberately, both of them turning away from the headlights. The wife drew her scarf tightly around her face. A red Proton Saga slowed to a bumpy stop, killing the headlights, and the tyres squelched into the mud.

A woman opened the back door. There was a slight scuffle, then another woman was dragged out from the back seat. She was blindfolded, and Colonel S could see the blood glistening on her forehead in the dim light. The woman whimpered softly, a plaintive cry in the silence of that deserted stretch of land. Colonel S felt the humidity soak into his shirt as they all stood waiting in the moist stillness.

Then the princeling tilted his head in a nod. It was as if the noise of the tropical night started as a simmer of twitters and chirps and flutters and squeaks, breaking the spell. Colonel S jerked his head towards the pole. The two bodyguards dragged the woman (she struggled against the soft ground which refused to yield to her splayed toes) leaving an anguished trail. Her blindfold slipped off, and the wispy black material crouched on the ground like wounded batwings in the night.

As he watched the woman being tied up, her hands and feet secured with ropes, the clouds parted and Colonel S could see her face. He had known that she would be beautiful, but he had not expected this degree of loveliness or youth. This woman had been loved by many, he already knew that but, at this moment, as the moonbeams shone on her face, he understood why she had driven the young minister and the princeling to such impropriety. He looked at the princeling's wife – a woman well past her youth, heavy in jowl and body, narrow in mind – her eyes glinted feline in the gloom.

He felt a moment of doubt, then reasoned that he had no cause to be squeamish. Colonel S – no one ever called him by his name, for his surname declared that his ancestors once walked with the prophet (Peace be upon Him!). His ancestry, coupled with his dizzy rise to the top of the military hierarchy after earning a Doctorate in Materials Science from the United States, made him into a Malaysia Boleh Hero. Yes We Can!

Thanks to the diverse appetites of the princeling and his cronies, he had the country by its balls. He was one of the main executors of the national destiny.

Tonight, he was entrusted with the execution of this young woman. It would not be his first, but she was a mother of two. He had seen women being stoned to death for sleeping with men – not here in Malaysia, but he had seen it happen. As he clasped the C4 explosives around her sweaty neck, he allowed his fingers to linger a little longer than was necessary. She was a whore, he reminded himself, and one *who knew too much*.

She probably knew too much about Colonel S too. He wasn't going to take any chances.

She had been there, in Paris and Madrid, when the cronies of the government netted a hundred and fourteen million euros in that submarine deal. Then on to Sweden where party loyalties were fed and bought for another of their projects. The princeling would swear on the Koran that he had never seen this woman, let alone touched her, but his wife knew better. It was the wife, calmly watching Colonel S circle this woman's body with explosives, who proved more dangerous to this beauty than the secrets whispered during any pillow-talk.

The woman stirred, murmuring softly. Colonel S found himself pausing, straining to hear her last words. She was from Tibet, but spoke seven languages fluently, and had come to Malaysia as a government translator. She had been very good at her job, until her competence and beauty got her noticed by the highest bidders in the government.

She had lived in a fancy condo in Kenny Hills, flown first-class to the bright lights of big cities... and now this ignominious end in a deserted field in Shah Alam. He refused to feel sorry for her; she had lived too well. She could be saying anything in one of those seven languages, but he didn't have to listen.

He felt tired.

Colonel S straightened her head, which had dropped to one side, and felt a line of drool on his fingers. His work was done. He tightened the last explosive around her right wrist and stood back.

One of the bodyguards stepped forward. He was holding a small revolver in his hand.

"There is no need," Colonel S began.

"Just making sure." The bodyguard aimed the revolver in line with her chest.

"You'll set off the explosives…"

"Don't worry, boss. I watch already, where you put everything. Sure shot, this one."

Before Colonel S could protest any further, two shots rang out in quick succession. He turned his head instinctively, away from the girl, and watched the young bodyguard's face in its malice. *That idiot aimed for her breasts!* He shoved the man backwards savagely, signalling for everyone to stand further back.

His ears, adjusting to the silence after the gunshots, waited for the warbling to begin again. The clicks and rattles, castanets and chirrups – the song of the night seemed reluctant to begin.

But no matter. He straightened his back consciously; he was ready. He put his finger on the detonator and the field lit up with a burst of thunder, spraying gristle and bone as a human being exploded into hundreds of pieces, the blood splurging out of a punctured heart. Then there was the smell of singed flesh and burning hair, as tiny tongues of fire licked the ground.

# Monday

# One

Agni drove along the pristine roads of a new township, built along the fringes of an elite golf course, its gloss reflecting a pride in appearances. No bohemia here to mar the landscaped views; only rows of manicured structures, trimmed and tamed, like all the expensive new townships of Malaysia. Her car glided along the smooth black roads, and Agni admired the mirrored image of cream and white buildings in the tinted windows. Everything glowed softly in the rays of the setting sun.

The Malay night watchman called out as she entered the lobby of the office, day-bright with the glow of a thousand bulbs. The marble floors gleamed as Agni walked carefully up the slight slope on her high heels.

"*Apa khabar?*" she replied more heartily than she felt.

There was a new Chinese guard at the reception desk beyond the main door. He held up her identity card and asked "Aag Nee Bee Na?"

He drew out the syllables of her name, making it sound Chinese. She should have been used to it by now. Jostling with *Dravidian* names impossible on the tongue, hers was too easily mangled by non-Indians. But, after having been an Agnes for too long in a small Texan town, she allowed no liberties.

"Agnibina," she corrected. Reclaiming the card, she swiftly swiped it to open the automatic door.

The cubicles looked like a maze in the semi-darkness. A low wall merged into a network of walls, stretching into long windows designed to frame the spectacular view. The wave pool at the giant water park across from the office building was switched off and the water lay still, reflecting the pink Moorish domes of the theme park hotel flecked with lights twinkling in the descending night.

She headed for the lit office next to her own. Rohani was

already there, staring at a screen. She waved at Agni with red fingertips, which had been dipping into a half-empty packet of pickled tamarind.

"Sorry for dragging you down here today. Hope I didn't interrupt a hot date?"

"Yeah... well, Abhi can deal with it by now." Agni sank into a chair. "So what do we have?"

"Not sure, *lah*. A lot of action at the airport." Rohani rolled her chair to the left to make room for Agni. "The security people are already looking into it, but meanwhile I just got these videos – taken in the last two weeks."

"And...?"

Rohani shrugged. "You see first."

On the screen, an old man sat facing the tall glass windows. The reflected neon lights skimmed over the chrome window frame and set him in a halo. He could have been a fortuneteller or a mystic, so deeply did he gaze into the night. The tent-like roof of Kuala Lumpur International Airport soared high above his head as he stared straight ahead, oblivious to the clamour within the huge hall and the clatter of rolling luggage being dragged to international destinations. The carpet was dense, blue patterned in the flying-kite logo of the national airline, and the background hum of the airport was a loud soundtrack.

Agni adjusted the volume level as she watched his left hand pat the pocket of his shabby *baju*. His sarong skimmed the floor, showing glimpses of feet clad in scuffed black sandals. The folds of his skin sagged below his eyes, but his wrinkled hands grasped a mobile phone firmly, the nubs of his knuckles clearly outlined.

The footage was very clear, taken on state-of-the-art surveillance cameras. She fast-forwarded to the next date, and the next. It was like watching the same tape, although he made the trip to the airport only three times a week, on random days.

He always chose a seat close to the cameras.

"And he's there today? Now?"

Rohani nodded. "The old fellow's probably just a harmless geriatric with nowhere to go."

"Okay, but how is he getting in?"

"No idea."

"I'm going to the airport, Hani. That old man doesn't look much like a problem but no point in taking chances, *kan*?"

"I'll come with you," Rohani reached for her handbag.

"Don't bother. I also need to check out all the strange employee clearances." She stretched backwards, letting the padded chair slide over her spine.

Rohani put the last morsel in her mouth, and tossed the packet into the bin. "*Aiyah*, I hope this doesn't spoil my holidays again. My mother will kill me if I don't go home for my niece's first birthday."

Agni gave her a wan smile before switching off the tapes.

# Two

Colonel S looked at his watch. The hands had a nice symmetry at ten-ten; it was almost time.

It had been two months since the Tibetan woman had been blown up in the fields, and the media frenzy was dying down. The French press published pictures of the Beauty and the Princeling, but the Malaysian press collectively ignored all 'rumours'. Only the bodyguards were taken into custody. It was unlikely that even the junior minister would be touched, especially as he made it a point to appear at press conferences with his supportive wife and that stony-faced teenage daughter.

Colonel S had come close to danger. He had been archly mentioned in a couple of early news reports, and even issued a press statement, but now, only the online bloggers were still interested in him. Thankfully, no one paid much attention to the bloggers. Those that got too smart could be locked up for-ever without a trial under the Internal Security Act, and the government made sure to flex that muscle as a reminder. How-ever, the pressure was on. Too many people wanted to see him make a mistake.

Colonel S had to move fast if the master plan was to work. The next event had to be executed seamlessly, at this airport, in less than a week's time. His experience made him wary of dele-gating any real responsibility. He trusted only a few people, not even friends. *Gigi dengan lidah ada kala bergigit juga... The teeth too, sometimes bite the tongue.* Especially in a crisis.

As the young woman moved into his line of vision, his brow furrowed. He had seen her before, this thin girl with the crinkled hair. He had an unerring memory for faces. Yes. It was the same girl who had passionately kissed a white man goodbye – when was it, ten months ago? – then followed the man with hungry eyes as he descended the escalator into the immigration area. Colonel S had impatiently passed them both then, irritated at the delay. She had a striking face, not quite beautiful, but unforgettable.

Why was the girl here again today? He squinted at her nametag reflected in the glass but could make out only the capital A, then perhaps p, or a g.

He focused on the way the girl concentrated on the red, white, and blue markings of the American plane in front, absentmindedly chewing on the edge of a fingernail. Without taking her eyes off the plane, which was now drawing away, she lifted her hands to the turquoise band holding her hair captive and, arching her back so that her short top curved up onto her bared waist, she retied her hair. He watched the way the pink nail polish glinted on her toes as she curled her feet into the edge of her high-heeled sandals.

His deadline-driven time in America, where he studied and worked for a decade, seemed a lifetime away. He had considered getting a green card and living in Seattle forever, but the frenzied lifestyle never made him feel like he belonged there. Giving up his alien status he came home, to a brilliant career in the Malaysian army, specialising in explosive devices that were compact and undetectable. He never tired of waiting and watching, for that was what he did. All he ever needed was silent concentration and time to execute his plans. While the minions watched in amazement.

Working with new biomaterials had been a team effort but, even in the lab in Seattle, he towered godlike above the others, moulding hydroxyapatite polymer and composites, mixing bioglass, and developing patents for biomedical breakthroughs that served as substitutes for damaged human tissues. He had taken the accolades and the frustrations that came with saving lives, and his last years had been spent on research for the ideal bone substitute. It still eluded him, as it had so many investigators in the field.

What Allah created was magic indeed; newly formed bone was strong, disintegrating over time yet simultaneously replacing itself. Only hydroxyapatite came somewhat close, with its osteoconductive property resembling bone structure, and its ability to bond directly with bone. Non-toxic, the human body accepted it, but it still wasn't like the human bone.

Working on different bone-analogue materials, he had moved to biodegradable heart stents: little tubes to keep heart passageways open and deliver drugs after surgery. All the problems with biomaterials were like a game of chess, he told the young faculty; your strategy must account for opposites, while focusing on the final goal. The stents must be inserted in a contracted state, and then quickly expand in the artery after insertion. They must be strong enough to withstand the pressures that a blood vessel is subject to and yet disintegrate after delivering the drug over a period of time.

Like Mission Impossible, *kan*?

He worked with a talented team, but no one more talented than Jay Ghosh, the young kid he had recruited. He had known Jay for a lifetime, taught Jay everything, even saved his life once. Unfortunately, Jay had too quickly figured out what was really going on in the lab.

But, no matter. Jay had been crucial for the breakthrough. Colonel S had almost given up, through the endless animal testing and then the clinical trials in humans, days and months when nothing came close to touching the finger of god. Finally, when it had all come together, it was a vindication of his belief, and he had gone down on his knees.

He smiled at the memory of Jay shaking his shoulders: "Get up, Prof! We did this, *You* and *I*, not some random god!"

It was a small matter, this matter of belief and disbelief. It was enough that Jay believed in the science that allowed such miracles to happen: A stent filled with drugs could also be filled with superexplosives.

So easy – this modification, so alike the drugs and the undetectable biomaterial explosives. A breakthrough so similar to the bone structure in the body that it could fool nature. Machines like the mass spectrometers designed to detect the presence of trace quantities of chemicals would not stand a chance.

Scientists with moral scruples need not apply. Even the money became insignificant when scientists were changing human destiny in a petri dish and, in that respect, he completely agreed with Jay about unfettered scientific genius.

And soon, the miracle would be in the warrior, who would sit on a wheelchair and glide towards a press conference at this airport. He remembered the crippled young man on the hospital bed in Puchong, while his mother wailed, "We sent you to be an architect! So proud, your father; now what has my son become?"

He had barely been able to disguise his irritation. The way the family was mourning, anyone would think the young man was dead instead of crippled. The bomb that had blown off the warrior's legs exploded prematurely at a shopping complex in Jakarta. But the warrior, just out of jail and with no legs, had taken over leadership of the group at a meeting in Puchong in 1999, saying dismissively: "They have castrated us all; what is the loss of a leg?"

The girl by the window was now pacing. He watched her frown at her reflection in the glass as a middle-aged Malay woman asked her the time. He drew deeply on his smoke, but his hands trembled slightly.

If the enemy could imprison their brothers and hang their

leaders, mocking their martyrs as they stepped into certain death, it was fitting that young men were ready to fight on the side of the righteous. Their people were in Kedah, Jakarta, and many places in Indonesia. The plans were simple: always lie low, hit non-Muslim businesses. They aimed to achieve the Islamic union of Malaysia, Mindanao, and independent Islamic territories in Indonesia.

The trouble with this country was the bastard politicians. The country needed men who bonded in brotherhood under one God, not the pimps that ran this government now, extending hands of friendship to everyone. The last two months, especially the death of the Tibetan woman, taught him some important lessons.

Now it was finally his turn. That pimp of a minister would be taken out soon, God willing. The betrayal of this nation was the most unforgivable in the hierarchy of treason, and it was his job to find those treacherous to the rulers, and silence them all. Colonel S had given up too much for this cause, remaining as silent as a watersnake swimming in this muddy river of a country ambushed by whirlpools, to fail at this.

The girl at the window walked out of an emergency exit, swiping her card on the door. So she was an employee. They must have noticed him on the cameras by now, and he hoped he had them scuttling. As he stubbed out his cigarette and lit another, he mused, in another week, it will finally be out of my hands.

He needed to call Jay. Colonel S wouldn't be able to pull this off alone once the plan was set in motion, and the first dry run was in a week's time, in Malaysia, but after that they would show the world how it was done. There was still a slight problem in convincing Jay to come back – not the money, which was easy – but in convincing him that this country provided the most congenial soil for any kind of research. He had followed his protégé's career over the past three decades, and Jay surpassed his expectations. Now it was up to Colonel S to woo him back to Malaysia, to take a sabbatical from the prestigious Haversham where he was now Professor.

He would invoke the blood-debt again; the ultimate ace dealt by fate.

Unfortunately, no one else knew the science as well as Jay did. Colonel S needed his protégé. Once Jay came back to Malaysia, he would be so deeply implicated that he would have to stay.

Colonel S could now see the girl with the crinkled hair on the tarmac, talking to someone. He picked at the hair growing out of the dark mole on his chin. He would give it another few minutes, then pick up his cane and walk towards the green and white sign that said *Keluar*. Then he would call Jay again, today, before time ran out.

A toddler wailed loudly as a young Chinese woman strained towards the monitor trying to make out the words on CNN. She shook the child's shoulders and yelled, "Quiet! I'll wallop you now!" The man next to them quickly scrambled up on one of the orange chairs to adjust the volume on the TV. Colonel S leaned back to watch the familiar face on the grainy footage from a mountainous cave in Afghanistan: ... *and they spread in every place in which injustice is perpetuated* ...

He picked up his cane and got to his feet. Someone with the logo of the airline stitched on his shirt started to walk towards him, but he waved him away. Then, with deliberate slowness, he extended his right foot, swivelled his right hip and dragged his left. People made way for him, smiling that pity which made his exits so easy.

# Three

Professor Jay Ghosh stood cradling the telephone in his hand, and yawned loudly. What an intriguing offer from his old mentor. If only he could trust Colonel S again! He had debts to repay, and that old fox made sure Jay would remember that by spouting an old Malay *pantun* at him, as always. Colonel S recited *Hutang emas boleh di bayar, hutang budi...* and, before he had even finished, Jay found himself nodding: *Yes, yes, debts of gold can be easily repaid; debts of gratitude are carried to the grave. Let me call you back in a week.*

More than a week had passed since the first phone call. The old man called again this morning. With the phone in his hand now, Jay couldn't believe that he, Professor Jay Ghosh, was actually thinking of going to Malaysia for three weeks. That he would say *yes* to a Return. That he would dial this phone now and say: *I will come.*

*Not again. Not ever.*

*But why not?*

Because he still didn't trust Colonel S completely. Research with him was tremendously exciting, but somehow also... tainted.

Because he couldn't bear the thought of going back to Malaysia.

He looked up at the ceiling. He loved the dining room cornices matching the flowered borders of the Turkish wool carpet leading out to the garden. This was his home now and, as always, he was comforted by its beauty and order. It had been years since he lived anywhere else. Then he looked at the lake outside, glimmering with chips of ice, and thought, I can't let a ghost keep me out of Malaysia forever.

That morning, after speaking with Colonel S, when he had stepped into the shower and seen the raven-black hair in the drain, he had jumped out, naked and shivering. How many more such visitations lurked around the house, ordinary human traces embedded in the couch and the carpet, the inner crevices of a memory that would not be exorcised? He had to force himself back inside the shower, to turn the hot water on and vapourise the images, but the ghost hovered over the soap dispenser and in the scum of the tiles. He had always known there was no reclaiming his space, only the certainty of sharing it. He had shared it with a dead woman for almost three decades.

Should he go back to Malaysia and make peace with Shanti's ghost? Shanti, his first love, whose mother had banished him so imperiously, but before all that were his sweetest, earliest memories, of a home in Kilat Tanah, the land of lightning, which two thousand years ago, long before it had become a Malayan Kingdom, had been a part of the mighty Sri Vijaya empire. Where the Thunder Demons had shaken the earth with incandescent ferocity before unleashing barbs of rain and smothering the land. Jay had lived his childhood within this ancient countryside where, after each flood, the river spit up stones, clearly artificially shaped, and he and Shanti had spent hours looking for this *batu lintar*, the teeth of the Thunder Demons, gnashed in fury and spat out over the countryside.

Although schoolbooks taught them that these were the axe-heads and chisels of the stone-age man, they had grown up with a fear of the Thunder Demon. The demon's teeth were especially powerful when casting spells, for age made them potent. Yet, when they had brought Shanti limp and dripping from the water, and she still had the demon's teeth pendant around her neck, he had ripped it from her lifeless body and sworn never to believe again. Then he had devoted his life to science, his work disproving the notion of any power higher than human genius.

Jay softly rubbed his fingers over that familiar bulge at his chest. He still wore the demon's teeth torn from the body of a dead girl, so very long ago. It was an albatross he could not shake off.

Maybe he had not tried hard enough, despite his twenties and thirties being filled with shrinks and happy pills. Maybe now was the time to lay this ghost to rest.

Shanti had a daughter before she died. The daughter, Agni, he calculated quickly, must be in her late twenties now. He imagined a face like Shanti's, but older, the familiar curve of a cheek at the tips of his fingers... he flexed his fingers into a closed fist.

No, this time, he would return because Colonel S had called. It was a challenge to work with Colonel S, and the last phone conversation had made that clear.

"Come for a month, Jay, that's all *lah*, the only thing this old man is asking from you."

"I have projects in summer, I need to try and reschedule things... I don't think I can, not for a month."

"Ah, come on! You have tenure already, it can't be so hard."

He had tired at incessant wheedling. "This is not Universiti Malaya."

A shocked intake of breath. Jay had not thought himself capable of such insolence and regretted it instantly. It was a relief to hear Colonel S speak again.

"As you wish, Jay. I just wanted to see you again. Think about this, please, I am an old man. I still feel like a godfather to you, and you, a child squirming in my arms..."

Jay felt his fingers looping circles in the air and knew he could not let Colonel S talk about the fire. "Three weeks. I can do three weeks. Maybe."

"Excellent! I look forward to your arrival. Somebody will send a ticket..."

"I'll call you back. Don't send anything yet."

"As you wish. Inshallah, it will be a pleasant three-week holiday for you, even if nothing else develops. But we are working on some biomaterials you will only have read about and I guarantee you'll be intrigued."

Three weeks. He would have time to see Shanti's daughter – he felt a warming of his blood – even time to see Shanti's mother again. Three quick weeks, and he would to be back in Boston... how bad could it get in such a short time?

He smiled as he remembered Colonel S on his knees in that lab in Seattle. For such a great scientist the man was a sucker for his God. He remembered shouting, *Get up, Prof! We did this, you and I, not some random god!*

Colonel S had taught him everything, besides saving his life. He couldn't have asked for a better advisor for his doctoral research. Their relationship was about work and if Colonel S was now offering him an open door back into Malaysia, he should grab the opportunity without a second thought for the dangerous research that Colonel S had engaged with in Seattle. Any research in Malaysia was immaterial to his American life; it was not his problem, and he would be back in three weeks. The people of that country, that babbling bunch who believed in magic and miracles, deserved god-men like Colonel S. If the meek were cowed, it was only Darwinism at work.

Now that destiny was calling him back, it was time to settle past dues, especially with Shanti's mother. It would be different now that he was no longer a boy. Living with Shanti's ghost all his adult life had been crippling, and he had had enough.

Jay yanked the curtains shut, enclosing himself in darkness as the phone blinked crimson in a stuttering burst of light. Someone had left him a message, but he would deal with that later.

It was probably Manju anyway... and he didn't want to talk any more. Or be persuaded *not* to go to Malaysia.

Jay headed to his computer, swivelling his chair so savagely that he dislodged two textbooks and a sheaf of papers dog-eared at the edges. He picked up the textbooks, forcing them between *The Business of Biomaterials* and *Ceramics and the Anatomy*, and then typed *flight time Boston Kuala Lumpur* into Google.

With the multiple stops on a last-minute booking, it could take him thirty-two hours to get to Kuala Lumpur. Even if travelling first class, did he really want to do this? He buried his head in his hands and thought of Manju. *Bitch!* He needed closure with her, and space between them, so that even if she wanted to come back, he wouldn't be here.

Childhood memories crowded into his mind: soft evenings like crow wings melting into the night; the call to the faithful ringing out over the noise of the traffic in a roundabout; the cadences of the language rising and falling like a happy song; his nostrils hit by the sharp smell of burning red chillies, followed by the sizzle of wet vegetables.

Jay's eyes watered involuntarily. He was getting old. He would be fifty soon.

He really wanted to go back to Malaysia.

The first thing he had done after Colonel S called was to search for Agni on Facebook. There was only one Agnibina listed, and he studied the profile picture, a cartoonish sexy Betty Boop, for clues. There were none. He had decided to send her a long message, introducing himself, and begun: *Your mother was my dear childhood friend and I still miss her. I have some work in Malaysia and will be returning after a few decades. I would be delighted if you would meet me. You must have your own memories of your mother...* and more meaningless shit.

This daughter would have no memories of Shanti, but it couldn't hurt to pretend. He read over the email, then hit *send* before he could change his mind.

Miraculously, Shanti's Agni had written back, a day later. And Jay had realised that life could get very interesting indeed.

Jay looked up at the oak-panelled walls. He could not think of a single person in Boston who wouldn't be glad to see him go. Picking up the phone, he dialled the Colonel's number.

# Four

When Agni strode into the hall again against the lines of the red, white, and blue plane blurring into the distance picking up speed, the old man had disappeared. She scanned the rows of seats, but he was nowhere to be seen.

She bit a nail absentmindedly. The irregular security clearances were definitely a problem. The employee identification system had been breached, and an armed intrusion into the most sacrosanct of public spaces, the airport tarmac, was possible. If this had been another stunt by the media to prove how incompetent her department was, she hoped the public relations people would be able to contain this in time.

Whoever had planned the intrusion had timed it well. The group of senior ministers returning from the ASEAN summit was due to hold an important press conference at the airport next week. Not even a full week left any more. She peered at the date on her watch. Time was running out.

Today's security breach hadn't led to a severe problem, and no aeroplanes were being directed to the Secondary Isolated Aircraft Parking Position, but the migraine sharpened into a pinpoint in her head as the phone rang again.

It was Rohani. "They talked to the old man."

The silence grew. "And?"

"It's Colonel S. You know, the princeling's right-hand man? He came to pick up a disabled nephew, some fellow in a wheelchair. Everything checked out."

"So why didn't he use the VIP route? And for the past two weeks... why has he been lurking around in some stupid disguise?"

"Go home, Agni, it's way past midnight." Rohani sounded tired. "Worry about the security coding and leave the people to the airport police, *lah*... This fellow's got clearance higher than you and me both, okay? If he wants to sit around the airport shaking legs every day also he can."

"Okay, okay. I know."

Rohani sighed softly. "It will be a long day tomorrow – meeting at nine, remember?"

On her way back home on the desolate Sepang-Damansara Highway, Agni rolled down the window to let the cool air whip her hair. Distant hills, an inky blue in the clouds, changed to lush leafiness as she came closer, chameleon-like beauty. She scanned the midget trees in the oil palm estates hedging the highway. In all this, in her childhood, she had never encountered danger in the darkness. Now, without being aware of it, she had started to see the bushes as camouflage, waiting for something to happen, the growing sense of *us* against *them*: *if you are not with us you are against us*, and she felt tired, sickened by it all.

Yet, there were few places better than this on earth. She knew, for she had wanderdust on her feet. She had travelled to the far corners of the globe with Greg before spending two years in Texas, but any other climate after this was too frigid, too calm, and the memory of Malaysia pounded hot through her blood and called her back every time.

The door to Abhik's apartment opened with a blast of arctic air. Clearly, Abhik had also just reached home, for the sound of splashing water was loud as Agni pushed open the bedroom door.

It was one-thirty in the morning.

She crossed the tiny living room, walking over the bars of moonlight piercing the floor of the darkened kitchen. Reaching for a can of Tiger from the fridge, she drank in great gulps until the beer ran down the sides of her mouth. It had been a long day. Tomorrow was likely to be even worse.

"Thought you'd be asleep," she said through the bathroom

door. There was only the sound of splashing water in reply. She felt like rushing into the bathroom and enveloping him in a wet hug, but sank to the ground in exhaustion instead, waiting for Abhik to come out.

She took another gulp of beer. Conversation was going to be impossible for a while, so she took out a travel-sized bottle of nail polish from her purse. She was sitting on the floor painting her toenails a silvery blue, smoothing on the topcoat that glistened like her moist lips when Abhik came out, a towel draped low over his hips.

His hair was tousled and his skin glistening, damp. He towered over her anyway with his height well over six feet, and now, contorted on the floor with toes cradled in her palm, Agni had to crane her neck to meet his surprised eyes.

"Hey you," he whispered. The tiny dimple on the left side of his mouth creased as he bent to kiss her gently. He held her for a while, breaking apart only to brush her hair away from her face. "Tough day?"

She held up the bottle of nail polish. "Colour therapy."

He smiled at her. "You have the most beautiful feet, B."

She smiled mischievously and pulled on his foot, still wet from the shower and sprinkled with damp hair.

"Let's see," she said, cradling the foot in one hand and dipping into the bottle with the other. Before he could react, Agni had slashes of bright blue on two of his toenails. "Now you have pretty feet too!"

Abhik recoiled and growled, "What are you doing, woman?" He pinned her arms behind her back, and the nail polish swirled into a mess of colour as they kissed and rolled into each other.

"Talk to me about your day," she said later, sleepily.

Abhik burrowed his face into her neck. "As shitty as always, and getting worse. Let's just keep my work away tonight. It's

34

getting ugly... to keep sane I've been thinking about *this* the whole day." Nuzzling her closer, he said, "You tell me... how's this new American professor you've been writing to?"

"Jay Ghosh?"

"Mmm?"

"Jealous?"

"Maybe."

She shoved him lightly, "Shut up! He's a friend of my mother's. So he is practically an Uncle, yah? He's coming to KL and I'll let you know when he shows up."

Abhik yawned, resting the back of his hand on his lips. "No time to socialise, B. Some of the Hindsight 2020 ringleaders are at the Detention Camp already... The princeling personally signed the detention order. They could be locked up forever without a trial, so I'm getting involved, in that legal case. Too much bullshit going on," he kissed her mouth. "Let's talk about something else. I want to know more about this uncle professor of yours."

Listening to her murmuring in the dark, he did feel jealous. Jealous that Jay had known Agni's mother, and her father, and that he might be able to put together pieces of the puzzle without which Agni felt so hollow. And he, Abhik, would never be able to do that for her, no matter how much he wanted to, no matter how much he loved her. Abhik let her talk, without telling her that.

Agni sat up abruptly, looking at her wrist. "Oh shit! I bet my grandmother's going nuts, and staying awake for me again." She swiftly hopped into one leg of her jeans. "Sorry, but you know how it is. My grandmother goes totally crazy."

Abhik caught her wrists. "Sit," he commanded. "When do we tell everyone? About us?"

He hadn't wanted to be the first to ask again, but it was ridiculous, her turning into a pumpkin every night at their age.

"Uhm…"

"I hate this! My family already knows, and they are delighted, so what *is* your problem?"

Agni put a placatory hand on his thick hair, brushing it down. "I need to be sure that – this will last. She'll get excited and… it's awkward."

"So what do you want us to do? Sneak around like bloody teenagers?"

"No! It's just that us, you and me, it's what everyone really wants… It's not like the others…" The implication hung in the air while Agni fell silent, thinking. "I tell you what – I'll talk to her, but after Deepavali?" She thought quickly, "Maybe we should go to Redang or Tioman first, some beach somewhere, and just relax for a couple of days to be sure about what *we* want?"

Abhik walked over to his desk and took out a folder from the drawer. "This was supposed to be a surprise."

The envelope landed near her knee. Inside were two roundtrip tickets from Kuala Lumpur to Bali.

Agni reached up and gave him a tight hug. "I'll talk to my grandmother soon. Really."

Abhik held her face in his palms. "Sometimes I think you wish I would disappear from your life. Poof! Gone!"

"Not disappear, buddy. Just a little more space."

"More space? I don't even see you everyday, and then it's like this, not even for an hour! What do you want from me, B?"

"I'm sorry." She kissed him on the lips. "Just let *me* get used to *us*," she said. "I'll tell her soon, promise."

# Five

Jay Ghosh felt the plane stop and then start again. Inside the dimmed interior of the business class cabin, he unclenched his fist and fought the urge to crane his head for a look. The boy next to him, perched at the window seat, was about eight years old, probably the scion of an important Chinese family in Malaysia and travelling as an unaccompanied minor. Jay found himself increasingly irritated by the ungentle bobbing of the child, who was looking out of the window with great excitement.

The flashing lights of the cars on the tarmac had distracted the child from the game on his screen. Now the control dangled on Jay's side of the seat, and he glowered at the intrusion. Jay pressed the button to call for a whiskey.

An Asian stewardess of doll-like proportions stopped at his seat. Before Jay could say anything, the boy screeched, "Why got police car and ambulance also?"

The stewardess ignored him and told Jay, "We have a medical emergency on our hands. One of the passengers seems to be disoriented and shaking. Can I get you another drink, sir?"

Before Jay could ask for anything, the boy leaned across and shouted, "Got bomb on plane, ah?"

The stewardess managed to force a weak laugh before fleeing. Jay closed his eyes and imagined Manju smacking the child's clammy hands off the armrest. She was the most unmaternal woman he knew.

Manjula Sharma... how had she come into his life? He thought of holding Manju in his arms again, but this time strangling her, watching the disbelief on her face. She would probably enjoy it, thinking it was some new sexual game. Pain was exciting; life had to be a tragedy and the constant pain of it kept her going.

"Every word, all nothing, day after day, it *hurts*." That was how Manju spoke while wringing a new poem, the single page crumpling under her frustration in the early morning.

"So why don't you do something else? Something not so painful?"

"Jaan, you will never understand!" she rolled her eyes.

Jay knew she wasn't his type. He liked his women smooth and fair, who never bared their arms in the hot sun, never breastfed babies, and kept flat stomachs and pert breasts into middle age. When they made love Manju clutched at him with a needy ferocity. Their relationship toppled him from the parallel rails of the ordered life he first envisioned in Malaysia, while swatting flies on hot afternoons and listening to the horn blaring *Pam-pum-pah-pah, Old newspaper, Paper lama, Pam-pah-pah-pah*.

On such afternoons, his mother had warned: *This is what you will become, son, driving a sampah lorry to pick up old newspapers, if you don't study hard.*

While his mother had droned on like humming flies he had stared out the window, waiting for *her*, the doctor's wife, his first love (even before Shanti, if Shanti could be called a *love*; she had been an *obsession*), driving to the club in her maroon Jaguar SS 100 Roadster. Her arms were hidden in a snowy linen shirt billowing in the wind and her face shaded by a ridiculous hat flopping about like the ears of her canine companion. Her lips glistened to match her silk *cheongsam*, and right then, at twelve years of age, he had sworn to become a doctor so that he too would deserve a creature as wonderful as this.

Whenever Manju started to whine, Jay sucked noisily at his teeth, dislodging imaginary food particles so that he wouldn't have to listen.

"I have never belonged here," Manju would say. "I am still asked where home is for me. I could be with three other American writers at a reading. We could have gone to the same school even, but it's so predictable; they want me to talk about *new ethnicities* or *brown bodies*."

"That's because you peddle it," he said.

"Excuse me?"

"Your ethnicity. What else do you write about?"

"I peddle my ethnicity?" Manju glared at him.

"Look, I don't understand it, but all this stuff about *others* and *exile*, and *dislocation*, and what's that word... um, yeah, *anomie*! What the fuck does it even mean?"

"*Anomie*?"

"You get all this attention because you are different, but that insults you? It doesn't make sense." He drew in an annoyed breath, "That's why it's paid so badly too."

Manju was calm. "If you think so little of my work, Jaan, why are you still with me?"

Jay shrugged and said nothing. She was *such* a bear to live with. Manju slept all day after working through the night, and was grumpy when awake. She was starting to publish by then, in small poetry magazines that barely paid enough to cover her meals, and she was teaching wherever she could, freshman composition if they wouldn't let her teach poetry.

Then she published a chapbook of poetry. It received wonderful reviews but didn't sell. She travelled around the country giving book readings to five or six people at a time; her biggest audience had numbered fourteen. Sitting in the darkened room while a spotlight shone on Manju, silhouetting her in a yellow cone and diminishing her sharp edges, Jay had been embarrassed.

When Haversham University started to woo him, he managed to get Manju a teaching position as part of the deal. He even found himself house hunting in picturesque suburbs with her. Then Manju discovered the press release that the university had sent out.

"The eminent scientist, Jayanta Ghosh; and Pulitzer Prize-winning author, Andre Parks, will be joining the faculty in the fall," she read out. "Twelve paragraphs of how wonderful you are, and what an honour it is for them. Oh wait! Here's where I come in: *Also joining our teaching faculty is the poet, Manjula Sharma*... the fucking footnote."

Jay shrugged, "It's a job."

"As if," murmured Manju.

"Maybe we can renegotiate a better position next year."

It had surprised him to see Manju gone the next morning. She had taken her things and left a note on the kitchen table. *I don't think you or Haversham need me.* He had been sure she would call; this wasn't the first time she had pulled this stunt in the two years they had been together. He had gone back to his lab, where his project on polymers in orthopaedic implants had consumed him. He analysed the samples from six resin lots of calcium, evaluating the stearate-free polyethylene for non-degradability. At least his work helped patients gain mobility, and decreased pain. He had no doubts about being gainfully employed.

Now, at this prestigious new university, he was in a different league. Untouchable.

He didn't have the time to moan about his demons, unlike Manju, whose fears were starker. "My father killed himself when I was a teenager," she had told him. "Suddenly, I came home and all these aunties were there around my mother. He had shopped around for doctors until he had enough sleeping pills to do it."

"I'm sorry." Jay didn't know what to say. He wished she wouldn't tell him so much.

"Yeah. My mother, well, she stayed here to give us a better life, you know. And she never let us forget it."

Jay had looked at the floor and said, "My best friend killed herself too, back in Malaysia."

"Really? How come you've never talked about this before?"

"What's to talk about? She got pregnant, drowned, left a mongrel child."

"What the fuck is a *mongrel child*?"

Jay shrugged. "Whatever. She killed herself on my birthday. The gift that keeps on giving, eh?"

"No!" said Manju, "that's so fucking unbelievable."

It was twelve days since Manju had left, and he wouldn't be there when she came crawling back. He was eleven thousand kilometres away, his plane pulsating at the tarmac of Tokyo's Narita International Airport, on his way to Malaysia. Jay looked out of the window at the bright lights of an airport that was totally unfamiliar, and wondered how different Kuala Lumpur would be, after an absence of more than thirty years. This short stop in Tokyo and he would be in the air again, then on Malaysian soil in eight hours.

He would meet Shanti's daughter. He took out Agni's email from his breast pocket, trying to straighten out the words.

# Tuesday

# Six

Diffused sunlight lit up the cool meeting room. The tinted glass windows looking out to the skyscrapers of Kuala Lumpur's city centre offered a spectacular view from the twenty-eighth floor, but Agni barely looked up as she sat shuffling through sheafs of statistics. The clients, who were government representatives, had asked for a meeting to discuss the progress in upgrading the information systems infrastructure at the airport. They spread a chill in the small room.

Two of them sat opposite the eight on Agni's team. A Malay woman engineer, who seemed to be in charge of the government representatives, was glowering with undisguised hostility. Maurice, Agni's American boss, had worked in Asia for most of his life, and was used to having his terse orders followed by people who never called him by his first name. These clients, who looked unpleasantly irate, puzzled him.

As the angry young woman fiddled with her pen, Agni recognised the insignia of an American university on the ring she wore. Another spoon-fed Malay government scholar, she thought dismissively, with a scholarship for being born Malay.

"Therefore, we will provide the fewest possible different styles and types of interfacing elements. Also, the information broker must be flexible enough to accommodate subsystems..." Maurice stopped as the woman held up her hand.

"We have not approved any of the drafts of the programme yet." The woman turned her ring agitatedly as she spoke. "But you have already submitted the final version for our review."

There was a long pause. Then Maurice explained carefully, enunciating each word, "The deadlines for your written response had passed. We contacted your office many times, but there was no response from you, so we thought..."

Perhaps it was the shrug with which he delivered the state-ment, or the condescension in his tone that made the lawyer sit up and cut him off mid-sentence. The Haji with the crocheted cap on his head softly said, "You assume too much, Mr Vossestein."

Agni concentrated on the way the sun gleamed on individ-ual strands of Maurice's blonde hair, setting it alight. The air crackled as his face gradually reddened and he straightened in his seat. Like a cougar on the Discovery Channel, she thought, spine taut with ferocity. He masked his sentiments under a smile and said jokingly, "We have had to *assume* much as we had a hard time finding your people."

"Yes, yes. Our offices are filled with *hantus*, our ghosts, so you never find our people," interrupted the woman. "We are not amused. You will have to try a lot harder Mr ah, Vossestein, ah, to justify your fees."

She picked up her bag, the Ferragamo clasp flashing in golden outrage, and strode out. The other two collected their documents and followed.

There was a shocked silence until Maurice laughed loudly. "That one needs a boyfriend. A BIG one."

The two men seated on either side of Agni erupted into laughter as she put her head into her hands and pulled her hair gently. Working with a pack of male chauvinist retards didn't help her stress levels.

She could understand why Maurice was scrambling to save face in his team. The Malay woman was obviously inexperienced yet in such a position of authority; as a relative newcomer in Malaysia, Maurice was still fazed by situations of competence being replaced by racial entitlement.

In order to get the government contract, the group had to prepare statistics in multicolour: green for Malays, red for Chinese, purple for Indians, blue for foreigners. To prove to the Malaysian government that racial quotas for Malays would indeed be met. Even if the Malay staff in the team was largely clerical, those tall bars of green marched across the screens of the boardroom with the assurance that the sons of the soil were employable, very world-class indeed. It was only when one of the tall bars became a person and flounced out of a boardroom that everyone seemed struck by the reality of it, of race and colour determining the destiny of all Malaysians.

# Seven

It took time for the ten thousand Indian protestors to swell to a mass of angry humanity. It would take the police more than five hours to clear downtown Kuala Lumpur, that too, only after the crowds were worn down by a barrage of tear gas and water cannons which sprayed potent chemical-laced jets into the crowd.

The crowd built up slowly, gathering in temples smelling of milk souring in the midday sun and ribbons of jasmine. Lunchtime idlers in the shade of the Petronas Twin Towers, holding out rice in banana leaf cones, pointing at the curries of beef and squid and beans and lentils, murmured to each other, only slightly alarmed by the growing crowd. The ice-*kacang* seller looked up, spooning condensed milk over the shaved ice and sweet beans, and briefly wondered whether to abandon his makeshift stall.

The protestors, defying three days of official warnings, had mobilised an unprecedented number of people, especially young Indian men, incensed at the lack of job and educational opportunities. They had finally mobilised the anger against the growing arrogance of a Master Race of Malays.

Without any warning, the first plume of tear gas whizzed towards the LRT station. There were distant screams, running hordes, and then the fire trucks aimed the water jets at the panicked mass. The man holding a tall banner protesting the destruction of Hindu temples doubled-up in resistance to the jet, mooning the police, but he soon fell to the floor. A sulphurous smoke made everything opaque. The protestors scrambled for their handkerchiefs, and covered their mouths while fleeing. Some people vomited into the bushes, others rubbed their eyes. In a clearing still untouched by the smoke, groups of young men were being handcuffed to each other, their arms raised in defiance. Slogan-shouters hurled water bottles and stones, then flower pots and shoes at the advancing police, before being beaten up and dragged into police trucks.

Chants of *Freedom Rakyat* and *People Power* started up, then died down again.

# Eight

Sitting in her office, Agni pictured the face of the furious Malay woman in the reflection of her glass window, and saw her ring glinting in the sunlight. *Bumiputra. Sons of the Soil.* One Sanskrit word divided and transformed, despite a shared history and culture – defining who could rule and who must serve.

One choice made in her history so many years ago, made on her behalf by her own grandmother, separated her from the Malay woman engineer. What if her mother had been allowed to marry the Malay man, Agni's father?

Agni rocked back and forth in her swivel chair as the reams of data, the letters and numbers, blurred into each other. She felt exhausted, yet the burr of the telephone was insistent, stopping and then starting again. The room felt unfamiliar as she stared up at the clock display blinking ten past eleven. When the phone started again, she sat up sharply, flinching at a spasm in her back.

"Hello?" The voice on the other end was terse. "Agni? Can you hear me?"

"Who's this?" A point above her left eyebrow throbbed dully, and she didn't want to play guessing games.

"Abhik!"

"Sorry, the line has a really bad echo... Where are you?"

"Listen, there's going to be trouble in the streets today. Stay inside, okay? Especially at the city centre."

Agni craned her neck over the money plants in the window-sill. "I can't see anything."

"Look, I can't talk now. Just keep off the streets. Trust me on this... love you."

Agni smiled at the mobile phone in her hand. Abhik, the intrepid lawyer, chasing ambulances before anyone died. The streets looked as normal as any other day. The computer screen blinked brightly. There was a new message from Professor Jay Ghosh of Haversham University in Boston.

By twelve in the afternoon it was eerily silent.

Agni rested her head on the cool metal of her table, thinking about the email exchange with Professor Jay Ghosh. He had unnerved her. She couldn't believe the things she had told him in her first email, a drama-queen attitude she didn't even know she harboured. It was as if a powerful magician from her childhood memory, a *jadugor*, had picked at hidden wounds. Jay had been her mother's closest friend but, even then, it was no excuse to have actually sent off that drivel.

Jay would be here tomorrow.

Agni got up. Besides her awkwardness about the Professor, something else did not feel right. She pulled up the blinds, and was astonished to see no cars on the road. Instead there were people, thousands of them. A lone police car had pulled up onto the pavement, as if to make room for the swelling crowds. She was too far up to hear the sounds clearly.

More people were coming from around Masjid Jamek and the LRT station, and she could see the Federal Reserve Unit and police cars amassed in that area. A group of men were coming down the road with a sky-blue banner, which had the Queen of England's face prominently displayed besides the words *Hope to Respect Our Humble Request and Rights*. The smaller Tamil words below the English were indistinguishable as the men marched past. The banner shivered in the wind.

Agni sat down heavily. Abhik had been talking about the Hindsight 2020 rally for months now. A Hindu group would petition for equal rights for all Malaysian races by the year 2020, as well as petition Britain to get involved in fighting for the rights of descendants of Indian labourers brought over to Malaya by a colonial government.

49

Politics bored Agni and, with the ASEAN ministerial meeting at the airport this week, the problems at work had kept her busy. What was happening below seemed like a bad dream; she couldn't believe that Hindsight 2020 would actually mobilise the Indians and challenge the growing Malay supremacy with this much courage.

How many would be killed? She felt her heart tighten; the crowd below looked like a sea of her relatives. *Where was Abhik?* Agni could see hundreds of them, men and women, like little ants being drowned in the sea of white fumes issuing from government vehicles, all of them struggling to keep afloat.

The phone rang incessantly after she speed dialled, but no one picked up at the other end. On the road, she could see three men jump up on a makeshift podium and wave Mahatma Gandhi's picture. A man with a megaphone started a speech in rapid Tamil, but was interrupted by passing protesters who waved a banner, *How is Our Future Going to be?*, chanting in loud voices. From her vantage point on the twenty-eighth floor, Agni could see the red fire trucks rumbling in from a distance, the BOMBA lettering on the side clear in white. Red berets, black uniforms, red boots. Agni chewed nervously on her lip and tasted blood.

When the helicopters started to circle, it was as if the faces all turned towards the sky in the hope of a divine deliverance. Instead, more chemical-laced water rained down, forcing protestors to their knees.

She had seen enough. Agni turned to her mobile phone and called Abhik again. No reply. She felt embarrassed by the silence of her colleagues, and squirmed at the prospect of walking out of her office and facing them, as if the shame of the protesting Indians was hers alone.

Even Rohani had not stopped by. Rohani, who would drop in to share every new twist of an office romance, or some fresh libellous gossip, had stayed in her room.

Agni absentmindedly turned on the FM radio. The home minister's voice was ferocious: "*Hindsight 2020 has said 'Our enemies are the Malays, the Muslims.' This is in some of their leaders' speeches. Yes, there are some issues involving the Indians that have not been totally resolved, but to say that we oppress, commit apartheid or genocide, and that the police allowed murder in Kampung Medan and Kampung Rawa? We don't want them to think that because this is a group speaking for a certain race or religion that we took action…*"

She felt a touch on her shoulder, then a light hug from behind. Rohani settled herself on the edge of the table, as if for a bit of gossip. They both looked mutely out at the scene below.

When Abhik called again, it was almost seven in the evening. Broken flowerpots, shoes, and glass bottles littered empty streets from which traffic remained barred. Shops were closed; only the five-star hotels had kept their doors open for camera-happy tourists.

His voice was exhausted. "Agni? Are you okay?"

"Abhik!! I've been trying to call you all afternoon! Are you all right?"

She heard him sigh. "I'm okay. The Hindsight leader managed to escape to London. He plans to sue the British Government for four trillion US dollars for the state of Malaysian Indians today. He won't get any money, it's only a publicity stunt, but maybe the world will pay some attention."

"I was shit scared, Abhik! Watching all those people in the streets…"

"It's over, Agni. No one's been killed, even though so many came out for this. Some Hindsight leaders are locked-up under the Internal Security Act, but the bar council is issuing a statement now. I'm going home. Coming?"

"I'll see you soon."

# Wednesday

# Nine

Jay sat in the cool room, reading through Agni's email again. Despite the warnings about the street protests, he insisted that the hotel concierge call a taxi immediately and now here he was, at Shanti's old home.

On the long flight from Boston to Kuala Lumpur yesterday, he had read and reread the email many times, trying to figure out how much Agni already knew. *Dramatic Daughter*, he concluded. *Fantastic Fable*.

Agni had sent a follow-up message, apologising for the melodrama in her first response. She wanted him to delete the message immediately. His response had been to thank her for her honesty.

Now he turned the page to read the ending again:

*As my father held my mother's head down in the depths of the sea, I sat at the shore of a beach in Port Dickson. I saw her bobbing up and down, her sari bursting into marigold balloons.*

*I've replayed that scene so many times in my mind. I can freeze any frame at will, taste the bitterness of the sand and the slime of the mud, and become my mother gasping for life, and letting go. For she did. She let herself sink to the bottom of the ocean, answering its call, and didn't look back at me. That is what I remember. Staring at her bobbing figure, I willed her to look at me, but she didn't even raise an arm in farewell. There was just a sinking, floating sari, and then my father returned, alone.*

*"It wasn't about you," my grandmother says.*

*But I know it was. I know I made it happen, for I was a decision; I was born of a fairy-child, both magical and cursed. So I knew.*

*We remake our memories in our retelling. I remember all this even though it happened long ago.*

*When my mother sank, this country stood still long enough to hear its own heartbeat. I could hear the waves crashing into my own booming race for life, while my mother's slowed to the last sigh.*

He looked at the woman seated before him. Agni was still speaking into her mobile phone.

Jay felt chilled. This was Shanti's daughter, he reminded himself; she wasn't Shanti. In fact, there was absolutely no resemblance. His glance took in the gleaming toenails and hair, skimmed over the hint of lace in the bared cleavage. He consciously straightened his stooping shoulders. More than four decades of his failure with women, and his shoulders were the first to surrender.

She hung up the phone with a terse apology, explaining that she needed to send a very quick text, but it would only take a minute.

Jay stretched out his feet and looked again at the woman before him. The crinkled hair, an untamable frizz, was pulled into a tight knot at her nape, which drew attention by its severe contrast. She could pass as Malay, this one. She looked a bit like his colleague in Boston, the one who had married the Pakistani fellow in a rain-sodden wedding last year.

Agni put the phone down and regarded him with a half smile as he tried to frame a question. She shifted slightly, the slit in her sarong skirt framing a shapely thigh.

Women like her thrummed with such tautness, he thought. Shanti had been exactly the same.

"Thank you for this email... and for inviting me home."

She shrugged off his gratitude. "You were my mother's best friend. It has been so long, but I wrote down everything I remembered. Maybe too much."

Jay smiled, even as his pen clicked in disbelief in his hands. "Yes, about your mother, Shanti, but... you said you were barely two years old then," he paused. "Surely, you couldn't have seen this... or remembered."

"But I did, Professor Ghosh. I can see the scene as clearly as I see you now." She made a slight movement with the tips of her silver-pink nails, and he felt dismissed.

She was clearly lying, but he didn't know why. Before he could say anything, her telephone buzzed again. Agni looked at the number and, with another curt apology, explained that she had to take the call. This time she stepped outside, talking urgently into the phone.

He was irritated by the constant interruptions. Even after meeting her, Agni's words didn't make it any clearer how much she really knew. Did she know that she shared her birthday with him? If her phone kept ringing like a hotline, he may never find out.

He walked over to the window. Outside, an expanse of manicured land fell away from the slopes into an untamed jungle in the distance; palms swayed in the garden, shielding orange-red heliconias bursting through the ground like strange winged birds. The house towered over the emerald landscape under an awning of delicately carved wood, propped up on cement stilts.

There was a swish of sound as Agni re-entered the room. "I am *so* sorry, Professor." She gestured towards her phone, "We are having some security issues at the office..."

She trailed off and the silence grew longer as she turned her face towards the slatted glass windows. Jay followed her eyes. Even though the light filtered in through the shade of a rambutan tree loaded with red, hairy fruit, the air was moist with the heat of a Malaysian afternoon. Agni's crinkly hair soaked in the sunshine and, as Jay stared at her with bemusement, she seemed to sizzle.

*Fiery Femme*. Jay reframed this woman in front of him. Fire certainly wasn't Shanti's style. Shanti had been softer and had sizzled less and, although time had dulled the intensity of her being, he still remembered too well. How clearly this daughter, this mere *shadow* of a daughter, showed him that Shanti had always been out of his league.

He was, of course, older now, while Shanti would forever be as young as the day she died. Shanti, caught in that vision he carried in his mind, would always be standing outside the house, under the old Angsana tree – shady and dense, where fragrant yellow flowers would bloom in large bunches, but only for a day. Shanti would stand, waiting for a bus in the early morning, clutching her books to her chest, kicking the dust at her feet. Suddenly a gust of wind from the east would brush the tree, shaking its crown so the golden flowers would rain down, and he, the fourteen-year-old Jay, would watch her transform as she raised her face as if to a lover's caress. Then she would twirl in that golden shower, bathing her languorous limbs. He would, over and over, feel that prickle as his friend disappeared in that golden shower, emerging as a lovely young woman in the spring of her life. He would fall in love, again.

Agni was waiting for him to speak again. But he didn't know how to play her game, at least not yet.

He reached for the *kretek* in his pocket. It was a lifelong addiction stretching well over three decades, and he had always found a supplier, even in Boston. This pack was half empty, and he tossed it on the table, the open winged bird on the cover with the *Gudang Garam* stamped below so creased that the paper flaked onto his fingers. He lit the cigar, and the sweet fragrance of cloves spiced with cinnamon, followed by a hint of star anise, wafted up towards Agni.

He realised his rudeness. "Sorry, do you mind?"

She started to wave a lazy hand over her face and wrinkle her nose, but then changed her mind. Inclining her head in a mocking request for permission, she bent down to extract a *kretek* and, with a practiced flick of her thumb, she lit it with his lighter. Jay thought her display of cleavage lasted slightly longer than was necessary, but who could be sure? Not that he objected to her charms; rather, it was the discomfiting notion that she was making it clear that she knew just how to handle men his age.

"I hope I am not being intrusive, but I grew up with your mother..."

"Oh, I don't mind your questions, Professor Ghosh. It feels good to be able to talk about her actually. Maybe that's why I wrote... too much... in that email. My grandmother used to tell me about the two of you, childhood best friends... your pets, some of your adventures. But that was before her stroke. Now she can't talk at all."

He already knew about Shapna's condition and the details did not interest him. It was enough that the stroke had silenced the woman, and made it safe for him to return.

"I was very sorry to hear about your grandmother. But your father... as you wrote, he came back alone? How is he?"

"Father? The Sylheti man my mother married, if that's who you mean."

She played with a thin gold bracelet, her arm glistening with the humidity in the room. Jay saw rich Chinese tea, sharp with the taste of gold on the tongue, and just a hint of steam. He flicked a silver strand of his hair from his knee.

"When my mother died, my father broke an earthen pot." Agni ground the cigarette stub savagely. "He let the water set her soul free, and wrung me out of his life. That was that. The last time I ever saw him." She lit another *kretek* and blew out a puff of smoke with great deliberation as the ash flickered down, spiralling with the dust motes. "I was handed to Dida, the conjurer of dreams, and her deep pouch of fables," Agni laughed self-consciously. "Maybe I'm getting a bit carried away, Professor, but you know how it is. *Thakumar Jhuli* must have been a part of your growing up too, eh?"

"That book, and many more."

But Agni's attention had shifted. She looked towards the bedroom where her grandmother lay sleeping. "Our grandmothers' tales are cruel, Professor. No tame storks to bring babies for us; our stories are about kings who believe that their queens give birth to animals, or that children buried alive turn into flowery trees to sing for their parents... so much crap."

Jay nodded in recognition. Agni leaned forward again. "You must know my mother was a fairy child, Professor? Her birth was like a familiar fairytale, but with an unhappy ending. No one even remembers the same story."

She leaned back on her chair, and sent the *kretek* spiralling out of the window with a backward flick of her wrist. There it was again, the flash of a tiny waist, perfectly dimpled. "Perhaps you should tell me what *you* remember, Professor Ghosh?" Agni dipped forward, her breath a whisper near his face, "Were you there when my mother died?"

He could smell the cloves on her breath. He focused on the glitter of her fingertips splayed on her upper thigh. It wasn't enough. In an instinctive, idiosyncratic movement that had plagued him since childhood, Jay felt his forefinger tracing agitated circles in the air with a life of its own. He had to will himself to concentrate, to click his pen with great deliberation. "No. I wasn't there."

Agni was looking at him quizzically, her head cocked to one side. "Tell me, Professor, what brings you back to Malaysia after thirty years?"

He frowned at her naivety, at the assumption of his truthfulness. When he had called her earlier from his hotel, explaining hurriedly that he was already there, this old friend of Shanti's, she had immediately welcomed him into her home. She was shaped by all that mumbo-jumbo which he too had once believed: goodness, friendship, loyalty... the munificence of the human being and community ties. He wanted to tell her so much, yet he had only just met her. Some things were too brutal to blurt out; he, of all people, should have learnt that by now.

He could begin by saying, a dead woman brought me here, but the conceit was appalling. She was right about memories being remade in their retelling. It was as if Shanti had been a goddess, with twenty magnificently arrayed arms, and each person remembered her holding out only what they wanted. Did Shanti's daughter need the saviour or the nemesis?

The silence grew uncomfortable. Then there was a slight noise of a door opening. Agni sprang to her feet with a smile. "I think I hear the nurse. My grandmother should have been up a long time ago. Please sit, I'll check on her and come back... Then you can come in and say hello."

# Ten

Jay watched Agni disappear into a long corridor sectioned off by souvenirs from all around the world. Grinning masks from Cancun and Nigeria were placed next to a preserved yellow piranha, teeth bared in death. He couldn't see much further into the gloom.

This was an old colonial building with high ceilings and cool mosaic floors, but the ventilation slats in the upper walls had been sealed to allow for air conditioning. He felt the soft darkness envelop him as he leaned forward into his palms, closing his eyes.

"Professor Ghosh? Are you okay?"

Agni was standing in front of him, concern creasing her brow.

He lifted his head and shook it sharply. "A bit of jet-lag. I should leave soon."

She looked at her watch. "I have to go to work in a while. If you want, we can talk to my grandmother for a bit, and I can drop you off at your hotel? It would be easier than calling a taxi, especially with the protests."

"Thank you, that's very kind. You work on Sundays in Malaysia?"

She laughed easily. "Not usually! There's a bit of a problem at the airport," she responded to his raised eyebrows, "but it's nothing serious. I need to go and check on the security system."

He wanted to ask about her work, but they had stopped in front of a darkened bedroom.

"Dida?" Agni murmured into the darkness, "O Dida?"

The blinds were drawn, the glass window slats clicked shut. The shifting rays of the late afternoon sun seeped in through the doily designs near the ceiling, falling on an empty wheelchair.

"Dida?" Agni called again.

"Let her sleep."

"She's awake." Agni leaned towards the huddle of cloth on the bed. "Dida," she said in Bengali, "Someone is here to see you."

Agni guided Jay to the chair near Shapna's head. The spindly legs on the old kopitiam chair were spread at awkward angles and he lowered himself hesitantly. Agni sank into a faded blue peacock on the bedspread.

A smell of eucalyptus oil and stale spit wafted up as Shapna turned towards him. "*Ke?*" she slurred.

"Professor Jayanta Ghosh," said Agni, adding in Bengali, "Ila's son? You know him, from long ago."

Jay had known that Shapna would recognise him, but the force of her recognition was startling. Her eyelashes fluttered like the wings of a wounded bird before she tightened them shut.

Agni let out a light laugh, while propping two pillows behind her grandmother's back. "She can barely speak, and her memory comes and goes. She doesn't recognise *me* on some days!"

Jay cleared his throat. "Hello," he said, "*Kemon acchen?*"

Shapna grunted softly and stretched out a slow hand towards Agni. Jay noticed the dark blue veins gnarled under skin that was almost translucent, and remembered how breathtakingly beautiful she had been. Her high cheekbones jutted out, defining a strong silhouette, and her hair, skimping over the pale skin underneath, still had more raven than snow.

He fidgeted. Her silence made him safe; he had to hold on to that. He wasn't going to let this slut drive him away again. This was the woman who taught him to flee from his problems, and he had been running ever since. He was going to be fifty in another year; he was tired of this.

Agni opened the blinds. "You were about to tell me why you came back, Professor?"

The challenge in her tone was clear – she would not let it rest.

"I am going to be a consultant at a research lab in Nilai... to work on biomaterials."

She smiled at him. "Ah, Transfer of Technology? Usually the government just pays for our researchers to see your facilities in Boston, no?"

"Yes. But there are some restrictions. It's... complicated." He sounded staccato, even to himself. *Leave Me Alone.*

She looked at him briefly before turning to Shapna. "Dida? See him clearly now? This is Ila's Babush?"

"You know my nickname?"

"Some of my childhood fables were about you, Professor. I know more about you than maybe even you remember, and about your father's work in that village in Port Dickson."

"A plantation, actually."

Shapna made some gurgling noises. Agni rose to pour her a glass of water. Shapna wobbled her neck towards Jay and, in the depths of her rheumy eyes, he could see her fear.

Slobbering Slut, he thought, smiling at Shapna. You're not the only one who can't keep a secret.

Shapna's trembling fingers raked over the bedclothes in uneven lines. Jay still remembered her, like an imperious empress, waving him away like a mosquito the last time they had met.

# Eleven

*I am an old woman who can't keep water in my mouth, Jayanta,
and my tongue can't spit out your truth. But I know that if you have
come back, after so many years, it can't be for any good.*

*You look like your father now. The same sharp nose, and his high
intelligent forehead. But you have your mother's swarthy skin
because her murky blood flows through your veins. What has
happened, Jayanta, to bring you back? How is that mother of
yours? Rotting in shit, I hope, with the rest of your plagued family.
My spleen burns when I remember.*

*You were my biggest disappointment. Even greater than Shanti.
If you look behind you right now, you will see that old picture, yes,
the only one of you which I couldn't bear to burn with the rest, of
two children grinning toothlessly, both holding hamsters in
clenched palms. You and Shanti. Remember?*

*I should have known. Even then, you would always rear the
murderous pet. Shanti and you would choose fish from the same
shop, and yours would be the one with the hidden teeth, the one
that would last the longest after gouging the eyes and the fins of the
rest. The rabbits you chose were brothers; but yours killed Shanti's
in a night so bloody it left deep gouges in the victor. Ah, you have
seen the picture now. You do remember. You asked me once, "Why
do I always choose the evil ones?" while tears rolled easily from your
baby eyes. I never suspected.*

*When you first said you wanted to be a doctor, just like your
father, Shanti told you, "Be a vet, lah. Get your pets to kena some
victims and booming business what!"*

*I didn't know then, no one knew... saving lives, hah! I thought
the real reason Shanti had died was that we had given her no reason
to live; and that I, her mother, was guilty. I carried the weight of
that guilt Jayanta, not knowing any better. Everyone knew Shanti*

had two mothers, and had been cursed by both. How could she survive that? That is what I thought, for far too long.

But your crime? It wasn't a vengeance forgivable by the gods. May your child die in your arms.

You are putting the picture back on the mantelpiece, lightly wiping the glass with the tips of your bloody fingers. But you will find no absolution here. There is no reason for you to be here, to breathe the same air as my granddaughter, no reason at all.

I curse the day I met your mother. I should have trusted my instincts and kept away. Or at least recognised the rot in her blood that runs through your veins. But I was so gullible then! I met your parents soon after Nikhil and I had first stepped into the harbour in Singapore. I was so open, so young and alone then, new to Malaya and disgusted with the languages that tripped up my tongue and made me seem foolish. When Nikhil said there would be two new Bengali brides coming, I couldn't believe my luck! I can still see Nikhil, sitting on the open balcony, waving the card at me. "Both Mahesh and Ranjan are getting married to girls from Calcutta!"

But the two brides couldn't have been more different. Mridula, Ranjan's bride, was a child, with pimply skin and an innocence to match her husband's open heart. Two thick pigtails looped with red ribbons framed a plump face, and she plodded in flatfooted. I pushed up her shoulders as she bent to touch my feet. "No formality with me, little sister. We will be good friends, yes?" Mridula was so shy that her cheeks flamed immediately.

But your mother, Ila, oh, I could see at once that she was very different. Closer to me in age she should have been more of a friend, but we stood across from each other with eyes that critically appraised. My first thought was a triumphant, She is so dark! – until I noticed the way her skin glistened. Even modestly draped in a sari, head covered in deference to Nikhil's age, she moved like a swan, her arching back regal on a gracefully curved behind.

Her jewellery tinkled when she spoke, so that the men, including Nikhil, turned to her. She looked at your father with an obscene hunger, while he found reasons to touch her frequently, even in public.

My husband was very poetic when Ila, in the middle of that evening, blushed and said that her family had despaired of ever finding her a husband for she was so impossibly dark, but oh, here she was! Nikhil closed his eyes and recited a poem from memory:

> I am utterly enchanted
> The sight of her beauty makes me
> Melt like wax before the fire. What
> Is the difference if she is black?
> So is coal, but alight, it shines like roses.

"An ancient Greek poem, bhai," he told your father as the men clapped with a loud theatrical Wah! Wah! Then Nikhil turned to me, finally acknowledging my simmering anger and gently mocked, "I didn't write it!"

I should have known then, to be wary, to never let my guard down. But during that sweet twilight hour on our balcony in 1933, when we were first acquainted with the two brides, poetry was quoted, songs were sung, and we talked until the morning. No children came between us. It was almost dawn when we finally slept, but I already felt I had far more to fear from Ila than Ila did from me.

Enough of my memories – you are here again.

Go. Go away now. I wish I could tell my granddaughter to keep away from you, but she thinks I only need water. Maybe I do; it burns my marrow to see you put your hand on the small of her back, fitting into her, just so. She is not stupid, my Agni, but she has led a life too filled with wide-eyed wonder, for I have shaded her so. We say Gacher thekhe phol mishti – Sweeter than the tree you plant is the fruit it bears – and my grandchild is precious indeed.

## Twelve

Colonel S dialled the hotel for the sixth time. He listened impatiently as the phone rang again and again before connecting to the front desk.

"Professor Ghosh MUST be in his room. Send someone up. I need to speak to him URGENTLY."

The receptionist sounded unflappable. "Sir, I tell you already, Professor Ghosh checked in, but went out... an hour ago."

"Rubbish. I NEED to talk to him."

He heard the patronising sigh as she began to tell him that she would be happy to take a message, and it was against company policy to disturb their guests by checking hotel rooms. That was when Colonel S lost his temper and pulled rank, barking orders to make sure that the receptionist and her supervisor understood who he was. He insisted that they go check Jay's room and wake the man if he was merely jet-lagged and asleep.

He vaguely heard the receptionist's nervous stutter about Jay asking for a taxi and leaving, before the realisation hit with a force that made him disconnect the call. What a fool he was! Of course Jay had come back to Malaysia for Shanti! Colonel S had, in the long intervening years, forgotten all about *that*, but Jay never, ever, could. After a thirty-year absence, after everything that happened, would he still want to see those people with such immediacy?

Colonel S had saved Jay's life, no doubt about it; even Jay acknowledged a blood debt, for if someone saved your life, it was no longer your own. But the life he had saved was of a castrated beast, still flailing about to make sense of the past.

Perhaps he should have left the child Jay had been to die in the stampede. He had not seen it then, but that rescue in the amusement park would spark the chain of events that taught Colonel S to kill women, something over which his religion and his conscience still stumbled. The killing of the Tibetan woman two months ago haunted his dreams, but she wasn't the first woman he executed.

That evening, so long ago. A confused child in the melee, red ice rivulets running like blood down his arm while he traced the circles of the Ferris wheel in the air in front of him with the tip of his right finger in a crazed frenzy.

He wondered whether Jay had finally outgrown that nervous habit of agitated finger circles.

That evening seemed to belong to another time. Those were the days when people danced through lives that seemed uncomplicated and easy. The lights had been psychedelic in the late evening, and the music loud; the noise from the giggling and flirting on the *joget* dance floor mixed pleasantly with the klink-klunk of the Ferris wheel that held shrieking children. Those days there was a lot of dancing in Malaya, and Colonel S had happily watched the dancers. Plenty of Malay girls, the air festive with colourful *kains*, extending to their ankles but fluttering open with their movements. Every now and then a girl would flash a shapely ankle in a pointed red slipper, extended like a provocative tongue. Diaphanous blouses glowed ruby and turquoise and amethyst and jade, and the long filmy scarves, loosely flung over heads and shoulders, floated briefly over their partner like an imagined caress.

There were so many butterfly women in the park with gossamer *selendangs* floating on slim shoulders, that it became a garden of dancing butterflies.

Of course, there was no physical contact between the dancers; that is what made it so delicious! The man would lead, doing his best to ensure that his partner followed his movements while the woman tried to distract him. He would try to edge her into a corner where she would have to follow his movements, and she, with mincing steps and an arched look over a shoulder, would dance away; no special steps at all, but the air sizzled with grace and promise and the excitement of a man meeting a woman. The music would be melodic, gentle, Malay.

He loved the slow rhythmic music of the *ronggeng*, when everyone on the dance floor seemed to glide, approach, then hesitate, only to turn a few steps later and come back again in a swaying movement. A teasing flirtatious dance, full of looks and gestures.

And Zainal, how the teenaged Colonel S had always worshipped him! Zainal was the centre of attention on the dance floor. He was taller than most of the men, and his black wiry hair matched his taut body, giving him a rakish look. His open smile lit up his face from within, and there was no dearth of pretty women catching his eye and making him break into a handsome grin.

Colonel S did not remember a time when he had not loved Zainal. Always, he had loved him more than anyone else on earth, more than his own father, or any brother. Zainal had taken him in as a child; Zainal was his King, his Father and, in the hierarchy of treason, *derhaka* towards such a man would have been the most absolute, the crowning pinnacle of betrayal. Colonel S remained loyal to Zainal, no matter what it had cost him. But Zainal had been betrayed by his own friends, the Indians who had come into this country to take all they could, without giving anything back.

But Jay was not like that. Jay had come back because he owed a debt in blood and that would guarantee his loyalty.

That evening, as the music was again changing to the faster *joget* tune, one of the open hawker stalls caught fire. There was a loud *phissshhhh* as the oil from an enormous wok flamed onto the awning circling the park, then the fire spread in the balmy evening breeze. There was panic everywhere: the gamblers and the dancers, the fortunetellers and the hawkers, the magicians and the children, all jostling and elbowing their way to the exits. Children were scooped up and carried, caps and sandals trampled in the frenzy.

Colonel S noticed the bright red ice *potong* melting in the child's hands before anything else. Then he realised that no one was picking up this wild-eyed child, so he acted quickly, lifting up the child who started to shriek with high pitched wails as soon as he was trapped in a stranger's arms. Then Colonel S ran, even as he felt the chill of the ice on his shoulders and face as the child struck out with furious fists, his wails shrieks of pure terror.

Zainal was outside, ashen-faced and scanning the crowd. He held his wife Siti tightly in his arms; his daughter was in Siti's arms. Relief uncreased his brow as Colonel S appeared.

Then Jay was held up on Zainal's tall shoulders, kicking and flailing, while the adults scanned the crowds for anyone with Indian features, who would claim this child. Finally Jay's parents, Mahesh and Ila, had appeared with their friends Shapna and Nikhil. Colonel S remembered how distraught Jay's mother had been, how she continued to sob.

Jay's father had kissed the Colonel's hands in gratitude. "I will never be able to repay your debt."

Colonel S had looked embarrassed. "No, no. Really... I did nothing. I am glad the boy is safe."

Thus began the long friendship between Zainal and Siti and the Indians. Shapna and Siti were as close as sisters – watching shadow-plays until late in the night, eating at open-air hawker stalls. They became Shanti's co-mothers.

He, Colonel S, had been responsible for that first introduction. It was because of him that Siti had sobbed into his arms *aku dianiaya kawan yang aku anggap darah daging sendiri,* that a friend, whom she had treated as her own flesh and blood, had betrayed her. Then she and Zainal disappeared into the night forever.

Colonel S knew the history of that friendship so well that he felt that this act of *pengkhianat*, the ultimate betrayal, had also happened to him.

Foreigners were like this, never to be completely trusted. They had allegiances overseas and foreign gods... and treachery in their hearts.

Colonel S switched off the TV, irritated by the same theme of civil unrest on all the local channels, the presenters couching the problem under phrases like religious tolerance and political adjustment. The euphemisms grated on him.

The last time the streets had felt this troubled was before the riots of 1969. Then too, the Chinese and Indians were arrogant with a win at the ballot box and drunk with hate, trampling the streets, particularly loud through the Malay districts and suburbs:

*Balek Kampung, lah! Go back to your villages!*

*Aborigines! Go back to the jungle.*

*Why should the Malays rule our country?*

*We'll thrash you now, we have the power.*

*Kuala Lumpur belongs to the Chinese!*

Mob violence was so easy to incite. Young men crazed by the tight swivel of a *dangdut* singer's hips only needed a crowd to make hoarded passions murderous. Taunts from a passing busload of Chinese and Indians set the Malays running wild and, by late evening, the first Chinese blood was stretching its viscous fingers across the road. Then the Chinese began slaughtering Malays in movie halls – the Rex, Federal, Capitol.

Colonel S squeezed his eyes until small pinpoints danced inside, flecked with red. The riots had come at the most intense period of his young life and taught him a valuable lesson; in a time of crisis, you can only trust your own kind.

Colonel S knew how to use people like Jay, but their relationship was based on work and nothing else. The difference between the two men was otherwise unbreachable. Jay disappearing to see Shanti's family as soon as he was on Malaysian soil was not a good sign.

He turned to the telephone again and punched the redial button. He listened to the phone ringing in an empty room.

# Thirteen

He felt Agni's breath on his neck and turned around.

"That's the picture of you with my mother? You both look so young! You left Malaysia when you were still in your teens, yes?"

"Sixteen."

"Do you remember anyone here?"

"No. I never looked back."

Her voice softened. "Then it's time you returned."

He didn't want her pity. He didn't want her to know that, more than anything else, Shanti had garlanded him with demon's teeth.

"Well, you should meet some of the old Bengalis soon. You've come at the right time... Deepavali is in a few days, and we still go to Port Dickson, you probably remember that? I can introduce you to the people who must have known your parents." Agni smiled expansively, "Everyone's family here; it is a small community."

A small community that minded everybody else's business; he remembered that well. "Thank you. But I think the only ones who may remember me would be Ranjan and Mridula. They were married at the same time as my parents."

Agni's face lit up. "Abhik's grandparents! Abhik's grandfather's been very unwell, and his family, they are everywhere now, but Abhik's a lawyer and he is here in Kuala Lumpur." She stopped and burst out laughing. "Sorry, I'm rambling! I grew up with Abhik, but you wouldn't know him. He was born much after you left."

He heard the exuberance in her voice and filed it away. *Amorous Abhik*? "I would love to meet Abhik's family. Thank you."

"Do you remember Port Dickson at all? You had quite an experience there... a fire, wasn't it?"

He felt an agitated finger tracing invisible loops and crammed his hand into his pocket. "Yes, a fire. At an amusement park. Someone rescued me. You know so much about me I'm feeling stalked!"

Agni turned, distracted by the slight figure hovering near the door. "Yah Zu, bring in the tea!" she commanded in Malay. She looked at her watch. "I can't stay much longer." Then, as her cellphone trilled, "Abhik," she explained, and hurriedly left the room.

The Indonesian maid walked in with tea and Marie biscuits. Jay's eyes rested on the prayer alcove in one corner, filled with the pictures of dead ancestors and relatives. The footprints on the white cloth may have been red once, but age had deepened them to a maroon verging on brown. Dusty beige paper flowers smothered the pictures of two old men. Central to the display was a sepia-tinted picture of a swaddled infant, the sex indeterminate, an enormous black spot obscuring the tiny forehead.

He remembered this altar to the dead clearly. This was the baby Shanti had replaced – he peered closer – nothing could be more ridiculous. There was no picture of Shanti among the dead.

Heavy teak furniture loomed over the alcove. Then the rosewood dressing table, elaborately carved with dragons and phoenixes that seemed to dart around the enormous wall. He recognised this, from another room, a long time ago. Shanti's dowry.

"Beautiful," Jay's mother had traced a dragon's fiery breath with an envious finger.

"Part of her dowry," Shapna explained. Then, as Shanti walked in, she added, "I hope my burnt-face monkey appreciates it some day."

Shanti ignored her mother as she glared at Jay. "Why are you sitting inside with the women today?"

But Shapna silenced Shanti with a sharp, "Go comb your hair *junglee*... oh, it's impossible to train this girl!" She shoved Shanti lightly on the shoulder, "Go, go now!"

Now Jay was back, sitting in front of the same furniture, sipping a similar hot and milky concoction in silence. Now the hand that raised the cup to his lips was lined with age, and the imperiousness of the woman in front was silenced by a stroke of luck.

Agni returned to the room and drained her cup in a scalding gulp. With the suddenness he was starting to associate with her, she leapt up and brought the cup crashing down on the fragile plate. "I have to go now," she announced. "I feel like a terrible host! You must come back and have a meal with us soon."

Jay rose quickly. "Thank you," he said, then looking at Shapna, "I would love to come back."

Agni kissed Shapna's cheek and muttered the usual Bengali farewell, "I'll be back." She turned to Jay almost as an afterthought. "My grandmother used to be the best storyteller in Malaysia. Did you know that?"

"I know. I heard the story of your mother's fabled birth from her, a long time ago."

Agni laughed. "Of course you'd know that one, Professor. Come, we'll talk in the car."

Shapna's eyelids were closed, but fluttered uncontrollably as she grasped at Agni's fingers with an unsteady hand. Agni raised her other hand and drew gentle fingers across her grandmother's eyes, pressing lightly, as if easing a child to sleep.

# Fourteen

The heavy wrought iron doors swung closed behind her. Agni waited for the electronic surveillance system to blink its good-bye before manoeuvring the Mercedes into traffic. Winding down the window, she waved a frantic arm to stop a tiny green Satria from hurtling into her path as she took the blind curve from her grandmother's long sloping driveway.

The woman in the Satria extended her middle finger, honking shrilly for emphasis.

"Stupid bitch," muttered Agni.

Jay smiled. "The drivers are more aggressive than I remember."

But Agni wasn't paying attention. She swerved into the lane inching towards a green-and-white toll plaza. Shifting gears, she guided the Mercedes through the touch-n-go lane, her face grimly silhouetted in the twilight.

Jay wondered about the call. Had Abhik summoned Agni to his side? She seemed annoyed. Well, too bad; he hadn't asked her for this ride.

When she spoke, Agni's voice was even. "After next week, this traffic should get better. But first, it will get a lot worse, especially on the eve of Deepavali as the whole country shuts down for the mass exodus. The holidays are a long nuisance every year, and the protests won't help."

He nodded. "It's good timing for the protests – with so much focus on Deepavali and the Indians anyway?"

She didn't look at him. "Any day is equally good to protest against injustice, Professor."

He felt patronised, but she changed the topic. "My grand-mother seemed very... agitated. I thought she would be happier to see you."

"Did she even recognise me?"

"Maybe you're right. She's been very mellow lately, especially with the new medication, so I'm not sure what changed. I should call her doctor."

He allowed a small silence before he said, "I am curious about your work."

"My department maintains the system security of the Integrated Operations Network at the airport."

"And that means..."

Agni turned to smile at him. The effect was dazzling. "Modern airports are connected by large information systems which connect a number of subsystems, like Point of Sales, Baggage Handling, and so on. The one at the Kuala Lumpur International Airport is called the ION, Integrated Operations Network."

She looked at the rearview mirror briefly before zooming into the next lane without signalling. "My group maintains the security of the ION so that the whole airport is connected. And, of course, working efficiently."

"So you are an engineer?"

"Um, an electrical engineer with a Master's in Computer Science. But on most days I'm the *jaga*, the security guard I mean, on standby all night in case something goes wrong."

"It sounds like an interesting job."

"It's stressful, Professor, especially as the subsystem that oversees the airport's security, and the surveillance systems, are my also responsibility. I have to be at the airport whenever I'm needed, to fix a software bug before it becomes a crisis. Even on Sundays."

Jay's tone was carefully playful. "Such odd hours probably don't leave you with much time for socialising then?"

"Not much." Agni switched on the radio to indicate that the conversation was over.

The traffic seemed dangerously dense. He recognised the

curve at the old Parliament House, and the landscaped Lake Gardens. They followed a trail of picturesque Victorian lampshades until they came to a standstill in front of the historic Tudor building that was Selangor Club. On the left, a monstrous plastic recreation of a Venus flytrap gurgled with water in the middle of the honking traffic.

On the radio, a local scholar was saying, *People are turning to religion because they have no place in the political debate.*

Agni turned down the radio and muttered. "I should warn you – the street protests might get ugly in the next few days."

He didn't have time to ask what she meant before the car drew up smoothly at his hotel foyer. She acknowledged his goodbye with a quick wave, before zooming down the tree-lined boulevard past the man-made feng shui fountain and out of his sight.

Whatever had come over her, Agni wondered, to tell that professor about her mother's death, and then insist on the details? He probably thought she was a bit of a lunatic, and she didn't blame him a bit. He probably knew how it all happened, so why was he asking so many questions? She didn't want his pity, or his nosy curiosity invading her life. Some scabs still hung tight to raw skin.

It felt good to drop him off at the hotel and head for the airport. He made Shapna more agitated than Agni had seen her grandmother after the stroke. She should find out why. The Professor made her uneasy too – she looked at her watch and sighed – but this job left her so tired that she couldn't think straight.

He was more handsome than she had expected. The childhood pictures of an acned teenager didn't do justice to the man with salt-and-pepper hair falling low on his nape.

# Fifteen

Abhik had woken up alone in his bed with the uneasy memory of Agni leaving in the night, and now, by midday, the unease had mutated into a dull throb in his temples. The roads of Kuala Lumpur were back to normal, with the detritus of the Hindsight 2020 protest – brochures, torn hoardings, discarded shoes and bottles – swept to the sides of the streets. The traffic moved slowly along Jalan Sultan Ismail for the next two long miles (as far as he could see), with the cars aggressively negotiating their way up a bottlenecked ramp at the end.

Abhik hit the steering wheel in frustration. Some fucktard had decided that taking that ramp at an awkward angle and jamming up two lanes would be a great idea.

This was why he got out of Kuala Lumpur whenever he could, zipping past the hibiscus and ixoras of the north-south highway, building an easy camaraderie with other motorists flashing their lights in the fraternity of us-against-the-cops. Tailgating the slowpokes in the fast lane, he felt an intense companionship with those who valued the speed and power of these well-built machines, a bonding made even sweeter by the certainty of its end. Inevitably, a grinning face would lean forward from the shadow of the passenger seat of a passing vehicle to wave goodbye, or a casual arm would lift in a salute through the moonroof at the fork on the road, making the perfect exit.

If only all relationships in life were so simple. Abhik drummed absentmindedly on the steering wheel, thinking of the bond that was growing, challenging Agni's silence. He read Agni's text again and frowned.

He couldn't trust her with an older man; she seemed to have a fetish for them. So Agni never had a father, but she didn't have a mother either, and it wasn't driving her into the arms of older lesbians, was it? Besides, being an orphan was different in this country where parenting was such a community activity. They both had grown up spending a lot of time at Pujobari, the Bengali property by the sea where, as children, they would wander off to the five acres of surrounding jungle with a bunch of kids. The jungle was dense with monkeys and snakes that trapped them slyly, sucking in a ball or pulling in a kite that refused to fly.

But, whenever they headed into forbidden territory, a nearby uncle would spot them out of the corner of his eye. Man, they were always looking out, even as they sat distracted, twirling beers. The children would be marched back and publicly humiliated as a warning to others but, even then, through all the tears, they understood that anyone in that gathering would have risked snakebites to keep the children safe. And they never forgot this sense of belonging. It still pulled him back to Pujobari year after year, now that it was his turn to watch out for someone else's kid.

Their grandfathers, and others of that generation, had pooled together half a month's pay to build on the five acres of land that became Pujobari. All the Bengali children grew up knowing that the dilapidated old colonial building was theirs to keep. He still remembered chasing small geese and chickens, cowering from the dogs, sitting at an open gutter and sucking on ice-lollies while some adult paid the ice-cream man who had phut-phutted into the property on an old motorcycle.

He and Agni had grown up together, but it was at Pujobari that they became more than friends. As teenagers they took turns volunteering for weekends of *Gotong Royong*, descending on the old building from as far away as Penang with rags and buckets and mops and ladders for a wild weekend of cleaning and camping, to be supervised by a married couple barely older than themselves.

The electricity blinked erratically, and the wind howled through the leaky rafters. Ignoring the bunk beds, the twenty of them had huddled in the central hall, playing cards until dawn, until a stormy wind through the bay windows blew out the candle. Then they watched the wind churning huge waves that crashed to the shore, bluish purple in the faint light.

Someone started a ghost story then, and Agni inched closer to Abhik, sharing his thin cotton sheet, leaning against the warmth of his chest. Sometime during the story, during the magic of the wailing night and the eerie drone of disembodied voices, Abhik had kissed her. It was a chaste kiss, mouths closed, a stupid kiss even. His first.

It was understood that the parents wanted such things to happen. A community gathering cut through the usual constraints of overnight gender mixing. It was only one kiss, but they both felt awkward. They started avoiding each other, just so that they wouldn't have to speak about it. When he finally had the courage to bring it up, he only said that calling Agni *Bonu*, little sister, as he had been doing all his life, was a little silly. *From now on, we call each other Bondhu, like friend, OK?*

*OK*. One sound in the Bengali alphabet, the aspirated breath of a 'd', renamed their relationship. *Bondhu*. Or Bondhu, shortened to B. That was how it had been ever since. They didn't go into that unfamiliar territory for a long time. No more kisses, chaste or otherwise, until Agni came back from Texas, alone.

A touch of a button and the window slid down silently, bringing in heat and cacophony. Abhik craned his neck to see the cause of the delay along Jalan Sultan Ismail, and cursed as an office boy on a fumigating motorcycle swung his way out of a certain collision. The stale odour from his body grazed Abhik's face and hung, vaporous, in the air. The mirror of the BMW now reflected the golden spires of Hotel Shangri La.

"Bloody fool! You fucking *nyamuk*!" Abhik shouted and, as

the boy turned nervously for a fleeting look, he added a few choice invectives in Hokkien.

But the curses were swallowed by the honking, hurtling crowd. The lone traffic policeman, with one sweep of his arm, parted the traffic in both directions.

Abhik wished he didn't jump every time Agni called, but he couldn't help himself. This old family friend – she had texted – since Professor Ghosh's parents had known Abhik's grandparents, would he please, please invite the guy home for the Deepavali party? They would all be in Port Dickson for Deepavali, but on Friday was the big Open House feast where everyone in the neighbourhood would be free to drop in at his house for a bite, Malaysian style.

He imagined mounds of greasy food. He imagined the slew of relatives who would ask him why he was still unmarried, and then try to 'introduce' a niece or a daughter, and he would be trapped completely, the ever-polite host. Although Agni spent most nights at his apartment now, she didn't want to make their relationship public. Yet. It was still too new, with too many uneven edges.

As if all this wasn't enough, he would have to entertain this American gatecrasher as well.

Right now he had more important things to think about than another national holiday celebrating gluttony and gossip. He was such a fool – but then, he could never say no to Agni. All she had to do was to pick up a phone and say "Hey B – take a break from that Excel spreadsheet life of yours and do me a favour, yah?" and he would agree.

He would call his grandparents and ask them to call this professor – he wrote on the back of his hand, *Ghosh* – and invite him formally. Meanwhile, Agni was probably escorting the old fart around town. The lights changed; he stepped on the accelerator with unwarranted savagery, taking a steep curve.

Yet, he reflected, he couldn't even name what he wanted from Agni. He had tried, more than once, but quickly retreated, abashed. Like their first kiss; they were more comfortable leaving things unsaid.

Abhik floored the accelerator as the lights changed to amber ahead.

Even when she had been living with Greg, he couldn't let her go. He was in England when he received that strange email from Agni, worded in a way that only he would understand as abnormal, something reflecting a deep unhappiness in what she had left unsaid. He flew immediately to visit her in Texas. He hadn't expected it but he and Greg got along, with the easy bonhomie that men affect over a few drinks despite the difference in their ages. Then Greg yawned, pleaded the excuse of an early morning meeting, and left them to catch up with each other.

Abhik got straight to the point. "You ok?"

"I miss home, *lah*! Miserable, yah?"

"Yeah. But I don't fit in at home either. Not that that's a bad thing... it would be so boring to *not* stand out!"

Agni smiled at him, both remembering the child he had been, one hand always waving in the air to catch the teacher's attention. "You always were into the limelight thing."

"Limelight? *Moi*?" He grinned. "Nah, London's great, but Malaysia's home, eh? Despite the fact that our government would prefer us to migrate."

She smiled at him, "And you get prejudice everywhere in the world..."

"Except in our lovely country, it's bloody enshrined in the constitution; no avenues for redress, sorry. And my family has been there for what, five generations? Maybe longer, if you take a closer look at my grandfather's photographs."

Abhik reached out to tickle Lucy, Greg's dog, curled up in a resplendent sheen on the sofa. "And you know what really gets me? We are the post-1969 generation. We don't care about the '69 riots because they didn't happen to *us*. But, with all the Bumi nonsense, we're all like – she's Indian, he's Chinese, she's Malay. But there are so many Chindians and the Malchins? The all-mixed-ups, huh?"

"You mean mongrel breeds like me? Stop whining about the same things, OK? We should just accept that here we are, two screwed-up people who will never belong anywhere."

"The globally promiscuous," Abhik articulated with relish. "Belonging in many places and in none. Cheer up, B, you seem to be doing all right." He inclined his head to the door that Greg had walked through.

"He's okay, I guess."

"Well, I'm glad that you are so exuberant about him, Bondhu!" Abhik leapt to his feet and knelt at Agni's, startling her by grabbing her hands. *"But if he ever/ Breaks your heart/ Before the next..."* Abhik warbled, off-key.

Agni had only heard him sing onstage in Pujobari before, *Alo Amar Alo* or some other equally vapid choir tune indestructible under the assault of childish trilling. Even he heard the plaintive tone before she shook her hands free and clamped them on his mouth, begging him to stop caterwauling.

Abhik bit the hand over his mouth with a gentle, moist tug.

## Sixteen

For Jay, the hotel room felt unbearably cramped after the spaciousness of Agni's home. The curtains were cheerfully batik-inspired, but the view they framed of the bumper-to-bumper traffic inching towards Cheras and Petaling Jaya was depressing. Jay yanked the curtains shut, shrinking the room even more. He yawned loudly.

He fell on the bed on his back, focusing on the green arrow on the ceiling. *Kiblat*, it declared, pointing the faithful towards Mecca. If only life came with such clear directional signs.

He felt himself spiralling into a deep tired sleep, thoughts pinging into his mind from all directions, uncontrolled. Agnibina! What a ridiculous, fanciful name! Did Shanti want her child to set the world on fire and name her accordingly?

Agni was still an enigma. He wondered what to tell her: How much? When? Would it be better to make her trust him, slowly, so that the end was sweeter?

She clearly believed that her mother was a fairy-child. He too had listened to the tale, so many years ago; yes, wide-eyed, sitting in front of those dragons and phoenixes darting through the rosewood, his legs jiggling on the floor impatiently.

Jay's tired eyes closed of their own accord as he heard Shapna's voice in his ear, narrating that fabled story, merging into his dreams.

*How do people deal with the loss of a child, surely the most terrible grief on earth?*

*When I lost my firstborn, a son, I couldn't see it as a celebration of cosmic renewal:* Just as a body sheds its clothes, so the soul sheds its body to take on a new one... The soul is timeless, infinite. *What use was such Vedic wisdom in the face of such intolerable grief?*

*I think I lost my mind. I knew what I had to do, and I did it every day. I set the table for the child and fed his portrait the food and, with every morsel, I reiterated my grief. My home became a museum as his gaze peered out from every wall, a macabre wallpaper that covered every bit of space. I sang to the child, I scolded him – all with a passion that left me spent.*

*Until the day Shanti came out of the mists of a turbulent monsoon morning. This was at dawn, when I was visiting the grave of my child by the sea.*

*We, too, have our immaculate conceptions.*

*In Malay folklore, rich with the animism of treespirits and waterwizards and bolsterghosts, long before Islam and the suppression of things originally Malay, there were spirits called toyols. These little beings were stillborns, exhumed in the dead hours of the night, and brought back to life with incantations and the sacrificial blood of a pure white rooster. Emerging out of graveyards, they had to be whisked into genie bottles so that they could work their black magic, masked by the scent of incense to cover the smell of death.*

*I had heard about these beings, for in Malaya the spirits have as much presence as mortals. Houses are haunted, ghosts rise from graves shrouded in their deathcloth, and thieves still use black magic to put a spell on a home.*

*So when my Malay friend, Siti, offered me a toyol, I clutched at the lifeline.*

*"There are rules for this," Siti warned, digging her nails deeply into my skin. "This one, it can really kill you."*

*That is how I happened to be in the graveyard, at four o'clock in the morning, as the mist hung heavy and floated past the vision in a dreamworld. What else could I do but weep in front of the earthen mound of what I had carried in my womb for nine months that was no more?*

*But then, out of the mist, out of that lifeless mound, there was a* sound. A single syllable that rose like a breath from the ground and froze my blood.

Ma.

Uttered the child. Then again, Ma.

The breath of the morning was so sweet. A hint of damp rain fell on my hands and I squinted at the moisture, willing it to be real so that the child would be, and I wouldn't find myself waking in an empty bed, the bolster damp with tears. I looked up and there was a child, gazing at me, and I knew it was a girl-child, not my son, though in the mist they looked the same. I knew then that my son had come back in a different body, but he had come. He was there, and so I hugged the child to my parched breast, squeezing out a sound of pain.

Long before the Japanese pocket monsters and Pokémon trainers, long before all that, this country had its own pocket monsters, grown in avarice and often in hate, trained to be unleashed at their owner's will. They had magic; they were magic – enough to bring a soul back from the dead.

And that was how Shanti came to be my child. I gave her a simple name for I, burdened with my own name, wanted my child to be lighter in life. I, Shapnasundari, as beautiful as a dream, named my daughter Shanti, a name that evoked the peace she brought into my life and into her new home.

My husband treated this new addition as he treated everything else in life – with a detached sense of inevitability. He reported to the police that a child had been found. Who she was no one knew or cared. In the poverty of war years, no one wished to reclaim this lost girl-child.

Shanti remained my magical child, one who was different and treated so. I had to make her special, especially as everyone knew she was an illegitimate part of that pure Brahmin tradition from which we sprang. So Shanti grew up playing on my heartstrings with her infant fingers, for she had given me back my life.

Jay woke up with a start. There was a gentle knocking on his door, and then a scratching sound as someone slid a white envelope under his door. He watched with tired disinterest, registering the padded feet retreating along the corridor. It had to be a message from Colonel S. Jay felt the ache in his limbs pulling him into a foetal curl in the comfortable bed. He wanted to fall deeply asleep and hoped there would be time for that, soon. But not yet.

He padded across the room and reached for the envelope. Tearing it open, he skimmed to an address in Ampang.

Clearly, he had been summoned.

The taxi driver seemed to have circled the periphery of Kuala Lumpur, trying to find the address on the piece of paper. Jay's watch indicated it was six twenty in the evening, but his body was running on Boston time. The driver wound down the window as they asked yet another pedestrian for directions, and slowly circled the greenery dotted with random dwellings. This was an undeveloped part of Kuala Lumpur, deep in the heart of Ampang, where the residents were able to maintain their isolation.

The taxi driver was a young Indian Muslim who wavered between annoyance and apology. "*Aiyo* Boss, all this new, *lah*! See new flyover here, big hospital there, where got last time?"

Jay resigned himself to a fruitless evening, and sank into his seat as the sun disappeared as if doused. He took a deep breath, and focused on the writing on the crumpled piece of paper while the driver veered into a small lane, squeezing through the muddy path between ramshackle huts, and shouted the address again. He couldn't believe his ears when the answer was affirmative.

Colonel S did not enjoy the sight of blood. He grimaced at the blood seeping through the wrinkles on his hands and down his wrist. Then, still holding the warm carcass, he looked into the darkening sky with relief. It had been a very hot day.

It was the eve of a national holiday, and the spirit of Deepavali festivity had crept into this little hut by the river, settling into the crevices of his careful life. He knew this city intimately and moved amongst the crowd like a fish in water, slipping silently and swiftly between people, stalls, carts; threading deftly between moving cars. With age had come fatigue, and now, with the media stories linking him to the dead model, he rarely moved out of his prescribed route of home-airport-home.

He had picked up the chicken from the many that clucked around the yard, pointlessly pirouetting in circles. He chose one both alive and uninjured, then, severed both arteries and trachea using a very sharp knife, chanting while allowing the blood to drain from the body. The animal had to be fully conscious until it bled to death, and he eyed the last twitches dispassionately, counting silently. It took eight seconds for the blood to drain out completely.

He squatted on his haunches. He gathered the chicken pieces into a battered aluminium bowl and turned on the tap, letting the blood run in rivulets into the drain. Blood dissolving into water. Even now, when he touched blood, his skin crawled like this. He squeezed the muscles of his forearm and shook off the droplets.

His body convulsed in a sharp spasm of coughing, and he felt the sudden wetness between his thighs. His body was getting old, beyond what he could control. He felt tired. He hoped Jay would come soon. He hoped Jay would not stay for too long.

"Yes?" A man peered out from the dark recesses of a room thick with inky fumes.

Jay briefly peered at the scrawl in his hand. "I'm looking for Colonel S."

The man appraised Jay silently. "Yes?"

"Is he here?"

"Yes."

It was hot in the dark courtyard. Jay felt he was being watched by more eyes than those of the taciturn man in front of him. He felt his ears getting warm as even the hibiscus plant seemed to shimmer with suppressed laughter.

He flashed his most genial smile. "My name is Jay Ghosh... I work with the Colonel."

The taxi horn sounded an impatient *pop*, reminding him he still hadn't paid. Jay reached for the wallet as the man turned to the foggy doorway and pointed, "There," and walked away.

He turned to pay the amount on the taxi metre, and added a generous tip. Behind him he heard a familiar voice, the English words clearly enunciated with a slight trace of a British accent. "Ah, Jay, finally! I was beginning to think you were lost!"

Colonel S stood framed in the doorway, his features unmistakable despite the gloom surrounding him. Jay strode towards him, one arm slightly extended, and the old man said, "You'll have to excuse me for being slightly bloody. I just killed my dinner."

When Jay's eyes adjusted to the dim interior, he realised that the inky smog originated from a small fire on a stove, on which a battered aluminium pot bubbled furiously. A naked bulb swung in a corner. It was the only light in the room.

Colonel S followed his eyes. "Medicine for my sore throat. Nasty inflammation. Sometimes when I eat too many chillies, or it rains too much, this happens." His eyes twinkled. "I should accept that I am old now. The only thing that cures my throat is this medicine from the Chinaman shop. Come," he crooked an imperative finger, "let's talk."

On a crude packet on the table Jay could make out the

gnarled shapes of roots, bark, seeds and dried fruit, and something else. He leaned forward for a closer look and recoiled. The bamboo bees lay still in death, whole and perfectly preserved, down to the very fine hairs on each leg. He could even see a few tiny accompanying salt crystals in which they had been sealed. They were fairly large black bees, with gleaming metallic blue wings.

Jay had forgotten the exotic forms that medicine took in this part of the world. "What *is* this stuff?"

"The best cold medicine known to mankind. Perfected over centuries of an ancient civilisation." Colonel S popped five bees, and the pack of mixed herbs into the boiling pot. "Now, while the water evaporates, let's get down to business. Drink?"

Jay shook his head. "No, thanks."

"C'mon – I insist. I have chilled beer."

A man stepped out of the shadows and handed Jay a can of beer. Then he disappeared. Jay shook his head slightly as he popped the can open; the shadow man, the bees, Agni... he felt assaulted by this country, and slightly dizzy.

Colonel S handed him a folder, "You'll start work tomorrow. It's not like there is much else for you to do in Kuala Lumpur, eh?"

Jay looked at the Colonel and nodded briefly. He wanted to spend time with Agni at Pujobari over the Deepavali holidays, but he remained silent. He wondered how much he should tell Colonel S about Agni. Their mentor-student relationship had been predicated on revealing only what was absolutely necessary. He knew that the Colonel had known Shapna, but that was a long time ago.

Colonel S was looking at him closely. "We're going to be running important tests soon," he explained, "A dry run, so to speak. I need you to start work immediately."

"Tests? How soon?"

Colonel S walked away to check the broth on the fire. "I'll let you know. Soon. You'll know when it happens." He looked at Jay, "Is there a problem?"

"No... I was taken by surprise, since it's a national holiday. Deepavali's in a few days, right?"

"Right. Since Deepavali's not a national holiday in Boston, I didn't think you'd mind." The Colonel smiled, "Kuala Lumpur's a madhouse now. All the flights are sold out and even the buses, especially the double-deckers with hostess service, get sold out months in advance. Deepavali's the best time to work, this city empties out."

"I still don't understand the rush. Why did you need me here so urgently?"

"Ah, my impatient friend, one hopes all will be revealed tomorrow. Or the day after," Colonel S stirred the liquid again with the long iron spoon, "and it will be amazing! We've been through much, my friend; trust me on this."

Jay took a sip of beer. He knew the old man too well to probe any further.

Colonel S peered through the steam, and watched the water hissing. He turned back to Jay. "I am very grateful you came... you were always the best man on my team. It'll be like the old days, eh?"

Carefully tipping out the shiny rich black broth, Colonel S deeply inhaled its bittersharp freshness. Like raisins put into water, the bees had swollen up beautifully to full size, and each bee was as large as his thumb, gleaming black and absolutely whole and perfect, the long wings glistening metallic blue. Jay's eyes widened in shock. He knew from his childhood that the Chinese ate the bile of bear, and pickled lizard as medicine, but surely, there was some concept of halal in the Colonel's meat? Colonel S carefully put the broth into a cup and placed it on a low coffee table in front of Jay.

"Ah, my mead!" he beamed, "My friend, I would offer you some, but there is only one portion here to cure my cough, and it has a ghastly taste. I can offer you another beer though. Or would you prefer something else?"

"Nothing, thank you. I really should get back to my hotel." He found himself making excuses. "I'm really jet-lagged, and I still have to call some people – some old friends of my parents."

"Ah, I'm impressed that you have maintained your ties over time and distance! I won't detain you then. But I was hoping you would stay for dinner? It has been a long time."

Jay stood up and reached out for the slim folder. "I'll have a look at this immediately. We'll have dinner some other time… I wanted to meet you tonight and thank you personally for, um, arranging this trip to Malaysia. I appreciate this opportunity…" he trailed off.

"Don't thank me with your words, my friend; there will be work enough later," Colonel S said. "I don't have to tell you how important the folder is, eh, some military work, that kind of thing. Let me at least give you a ride to this hotel of yours. It's impossible to get a taxi to come in here with all the trouble on the streets! Let me have my man drive you back safely with this folder, and we will talk again soon."

He enveloped Jay in a half hug. Then, stepping slightly back, he said, "I am so glad to see you. Welcome back!"

# Thursday

## Seventeen

Agni's eyes burned from checking and rechecking the subsystems. Blurry data still scrolled across multiple screens. When the call came in, she automatically picked up the phone, leaned back, and shut her eyes tight.

It was Jay. Of course, it was the Professor.

She *had* been a bit rude to him yesterday, but the memory of Shapna's distress made her head pulse at his cheery, "Hul-lo, is this a bad time to call?"

She forced her voice to remain even. "No, it's fine. You caught me by surprise, that's all. How are you? Jet-lagged?"

"No, I'm good now. Um, I was hoping you would have time to have some coffee with me today? I have to start work soon, at this research lab in Nilai, but I wanted to talk to you again. For old time's sake and, um, we didn't really get to talk much... about anything..."

She heard the nervousness in his voice. Maybe he was always like that; or there was something important he wanted to say. She wondered whether to tell him that he was invited to Abhik's house tomorrow and she could talk to him there. But that would be such a brush-off. Besides, it would be impossible to ask him any personal questions about her mother or father in that large gathering.

It would be better to find out what he wanted from her, and get that over and done with. And get out of this office at the same time. She looked at her watch, "Had lunch yet?"

"Nope. I slept through breakfast too."

"Join me for a quick lunch then? I have to pick up a blouse from my tailor at Semua House, and I was planning to eat at the hawker stalls around there. If you don't mind, that is?"

"Sounds great."

"I have to warn you... the place will be crawling with people."

"I spent my childhood here, remember?"

She paused briefly. "Right. How about I pick you up from your hotel lobby in about twenty minutes? I'm not very far."

She had dark patches under her eyes. Jay couldn't decide whether it was due to the liberal amounts of *kohl* she used, or a late night. Agni sat framed by palms in a deep winged armchair as the blue expanse of the swimming pool stretched out behind her. One foot idly circled the air while she turned the page of a magazine. Today, Jay noticed with pleasure, she was in tailored pants with a cropped top that played peek-a-boo with her bare midriff. A light blue jacket was slung casually on the armrest.

*Clearly the Cool Coquette.*

"Thanks for stopping by. I'm afraid I'm being a nuisance but you are very kind."

Agni shook her head. "It's ok. I had an awful meeting in the morning and it's good to get away from the post-mortem." She fished out a ticket, and led the way across the plush carpeting of the hotel's lobby and outside to the silver Mercedes. As she draped herself over the valet's podium to give him a tip, she said something to the young attendant in Malay that caused him to wink cheekily at her. Jay stood there, catching a phrase or two, but missing the message.

"Remember any Malay?" Agni asked.

He smiled ruefully, "*Sikit, Sikit.*"

She smiled, "Maybe it will come back. You'll be fine with English, of course."

"I thought so, but a receptionist yesterday was monolingual. She had to call someone else."

He lowered himself into the car, and Agni sighed. Déjà vu. So often, with Greg, she had felt that she was constantly translating. Greg had lived in Malaysia for a little over a year, but the alliances, especially the overt politeness and hidden resentments, never failed to shock him when he encountered them. And she had wearied of playing the interpreter of the inexplicable. Greg thought he needed to adjudicate in the Malaysian squabbling, and he was always wrong, until the Malaysians had nicknamed him a *Blur Sotong*, a squid with desperately waving tentacles that blurred the reality around him.

Agni looked obliquely at this other American seated next to her. She hoped Jay wouldn't need too much hand-holding before he left. He was undoubtedly a dear friend of her mother's, but she didn't have time to play tourist guide.

Hindi music blared from the shops in Jalan Masjid India. It was a cacophony of similar sounds with throbbing basses. Jay couldn't hear any Malay music.

He stopped to listen to the familiar Hindi tunes in disbelief. Agni laughed. "*Kuch Kuch Hota Hai* was the youth anthem in this country," she explained. "Last Hari Raya, the government had to ask the TV stations to show Malay movies on a Muslim holiday, instead of all these Hindi movies that are so popular. The Malay kids are crazy about Bollywood, and especially King Khan!"

While Agni was whisked up in an ancient elevator, Jay browsed the colourful pavement displays that hawked everything from prayer caps to male potency pills. She soon reappeared, triumphantly holding a thin plastic bag, exulting at her success in getting her blouse from the tailor without having to make repeated trips.

"Shall we?" she gestured with her head towards an area heavy with the aroma of spices.

The hawker stalls jostled each other in congested congeniality. They ordered some *lobak* and *popiah* from a Chinese stall, and then munched on *satay* and *murtabak* from the Malay stall next door. Jay watched Agni as she reached for her glass of Kopi-O and stirred the concoction with a long metal spoon. Then she picked up a flimsy pink plastic straw, put a finger over the top, filled it with liquid from her glass, and turned the straw over to let the liquid run out into the road.

A dim memory ran through his head. "That's really not very hygienic, you know," he finally commented. "If the straw is dirty, cleaning the inside of it with your coffee doesn't help. The germs are probably on the outside."

"Thanks for the lecture, Prof." Agni screwed up her nose at him. "It's a ritual. I doubt we Malaysians drink this stuff any other way."

"Ritual, huh? Like the way you just opened a new cigarette pack and turned one upside down? I was wondering about that."

Agni grinned. "Are you watching me too closely, Prof?"

He felt his ears grow hot. They ate quietly for a while, Jay reaching for the dimpled pink napkins. The heat and the spice seemed to gently fry his head. Agni didn't seem affected at all, except for a slight sheen of sweat on her upper lip.

"So, tell me something about my mother."

Jay had to collect his thoughts. "Shanti? We were very good friends."

Agni looked at him steadily. "I am not stupid, Professor. You agitated my grandmother more than anyone else she has seen since the stroke."

He was disarmed by her directness, veiling a hint of steel. He would have to tread carefully. This was Shapna's granddaughter, and Shapna had been a wounded tigress in defending her clan.

"I remind her of Shanti. And Shanti caused her a great deal of pain. Isn't that enough reason?"

It felt childish, the way he had to stare her down. Finally she looked away and laughed self-consciously, "Maybe I'm getting carried away, but I grew up with the whispered secrets that were mine by heritage. The heritage of the bastard child... I was hoping you would tell me something I didn't already know."

"Oh come on... *bastard* child?"

"Surely you know my father was Malay? My birth came as a death sentence to my mother. You know this; you were there."

He stirred uncomfortably. How much did she know? "I thought you said your father was Sylheti."

"Pay attention, Prof. I said he was the man my mother married." A slight smile took away the sting of her words. "Nobody ever talks to me about my real father, but I know he was Malay. I know that my grandmother went on about the shame of being a second wife, of having to embrace Islam in order to marry a Muslim in this country. *We will not have any rights over your dead body; why don't you just kill yourself now?* – that kind of thing. So my mother did."

"And how can you know this? You were a baby when your mother died."

She rolled her eyes. "A cousin first said something. Then when I was thirteen, and thought I was falling in love with a Bengali boy, there were whispers at Pujobari designed to be overheard by the bastard child... that sort of thing."

"Did you ever look for your father?"

"No. His name wasn't even spat out in anger in my family. Only his race and religion mattered; everything else is immaterial." Agni stirred her drink gently, not looking up. "I think my father was Zainal. His wife, Siti, was my grandmother's best friend."

He felt his fingers tracing agitated circles under the table as he searched for ways to deal with such a frontal assault.

Agni continued, "So. No more half-truths. I want you to tell me about my father, Professor," she urged. "No one ever talks about him. At least you have been asking me questions about my mother... no one does that. I want to know what my father was like."

Her hair shielded her face as she drank. It was impossible to see the expression on her face.

"How long have you known this?" he asked.

"Actually, I think I always suspected it. All the whispering in Pujobari... He must have been much older?"

"Thirty-three years older than Shanti."

He almost heard Agni calculating rapidly.

"So what did she see in him?" Agni asked.

*Where do I begin?* "Zainal was a great hero... an amazing man," Jay said simply. "When he told his stories, it was hard not to fall in love with him."

# Eighteen

Even he, Jay told Agni, had been a little in love with Zainal. As a boy, Jay hero-worshipped Zainal through the Emergency Years.

The Malayan Emergency lasted twelve long years. All over Malaysia, in the evenings, families would switch off lights and cower on the floors. The signal to do so would not be the sirens of war, but the dull thud of boots indicating the communists, most of them Chinese, were lurking in the dark. As they listened on the radio to the dramatic success of communism in China, the communists in Malaya set themselves up and grew stronger in the jungles of the neighbourhood.

Zainal was one of the first to volunteer to fight the communists. Twelve years worth of stories of Zainal's heroism, as both Shanti and Jay grew up. Zainal was a tall man and, illuminated by the small light in the post-dinner storytelling sessions, his shadow would loom even larger on the wall. His stories would flow into the night, sometimes stretching into dawn. During the years of the Emergency, they heard many stories of Zainal running into large bandit camps and exchanging bursts of gunfire in the thick jungle. But his most dramatic story, by far, was the capture of the Kajang Terror.

The Kajang Terror prowled the district of Selangor but, despite the reward of twenty-five thousand on his head, the people of the villages and *kampungs* in his area feared him. He was a legend. He operated around Sungei Besi, Serdang, and the Kuala Langat Forest Reserve, but his favourite areas were around Kajang and Banting, and the jungle swamps in between these two towns. He massacred the troops and the police who got in his way, for he had many thousands of Min Yuen and other informers working for him.

"So how did you track him down?" Shanti asked Zainal one evening.

A wind blew through the light, making shadows waver. Jay covered his mouth to stifle a tired yawn and closed his eyes, while his ears sharpened for the murmuring voices. Zainal cracked his knuckles slowly, one by one, and then, after the suspense had stretched the room taut with its silence, he began his story.

"First, we try and follow the tracks to the edge of the swamp, but we lose them to the leeches and the snakes and centipedes."

Zainal ruffled the hair of his youngest child and said, "*Aiyoh, even the centipede's not as troublesome as the little nyamuk*," with a meaningful smile at his little son. The little mosquitoes, he explained, caused the most trouble in the jungle. They had to keep their faces and hands covered with a sarong, with only the eyes and the nose sticking out.

Drawn into the wilderness by Zainal's voice, the young Jay could see the pale faces of the bandits moving through the dense undergrowth carefully, using hand signals to communicate. The jungle was deathly quiet during the day, and sounds and smells could be detected quite easily by a wary patrol. The rainforest was beautiful, with thousands of tall trees, white, grey, and shaded with almost every colour imaginable, all reaching towards the sunlight, hundreds of feet up. There, they spread out in a carpet of tangled green as the creepers, rattans, and vines hung down from the trees. No birds could be seen, for they were above the canopy in the bright sunlight. The light in the deep jungle was very faint, distilled through the ancient trees, and the air was moist with the breath of their long existence.

The day Zainal's platoon captured the Kajang Terror, the call had come from Bukit Hitam Estate, about three bandits trying to collect protection money from rubber tappers. The men got into two trucks, and circled round and round the hill dense with rubber trees.

"Then the *krackkrackkrack* Bren gun fire *zoooom* past my left ear. I duck, but the ground near the bush is bloody, and blood trickling down the fallen leaves of the rubber trees. *Alhamdulillah*, I was safe! Although a bandit with a grenade is right next to me, planning to throw grenade, someone empty a gun from close range into him!"

Siti never asked Zainal any questions. But Jay could see her lips moving in the lamplight, and she stared at Zainal's fingers as he squeezed together a thumb and forefinger to illustrate his narrow escape.

Zainal's troop had followed the small jungle track and, after walking about fifty yards, suddenly heard music. In a small clearing there was a rustic hut, and inside was a radio.

"Playing dum-da-da-dah, so we know that the time was exactly nine in the morning. We start to close in, quietly, very, very quietly. Three bandits come out; one with long beard, like this, and one a girl, all with guns and uniforms some more. So we open fire, *lah*, and the bandits ran, all of them from the hut and jump into the swamp. The Kajang Terror by this time was fat, really fat, and suddenly there he was, stuck in the swamp like a hippo. Somebody fire and *pshew*, straight through the eye, and The Terror was dead. It all happen so fast no time to think also."

They brought the body into Klang and tied him to a wooden door; then trailed the corpse behind a police van, for all the Min Yuen and other Chinese fellows to see and learn. They went to all the towns and *kampung* areas the bandits had previously terrorised, so that the people would know that the legend had ended... that he was really dead.

"But these people, so stupid one. Really afraid of him, think his *hantu* is even more powerful now that he is dead. Even the Malays, they sit in mosques and talk about this ghost that never die," Zainal shook his head.

Jay remembered Shanti sitting still after this story, absorbed in her own thoughts. His heart had cramped as Shapna looked at her watch irritably and signalled that it was time to go home. Siti, Zainal's wife, had kissed Shanti on the forehead in goodbye.

Siti had loved Shanti like a daughter. She and Shapna conjured Shanti out of a bottle (they claimed) and both loved her equally. He still had a picture, in Boston, which showed Siti looking lovingly at Shanti as she lay curled against the cushions, scribbling into a notebook balanced on her knees. *If the seed is good, when it falls into the ocean an island will spring up*; that was what Siti said when Jay took that picture.

But Shanti died for them the day she found her soulmate.

Zainal was thirty-three years older than her. Yet, she had found sanity in his arms, and contentment in the knowledge that his religion allowed him more than one wife.

For Siti, her husband's infidelity came as a shadow-play on the kitchen wall.

The night was cool, and Shanti and Jay were spending the evening at Siti's house again. The TV droned on, as usual.

Shanti got up to get some water. Zainal followed. Siti, looking up from the TV, wondered at the long silence, listened for the drip of the tap, the clink of a glass, but heard nothing. Instead, two shadows on the kitchen wall merged soundlessly. The shadows heightened as he pulled away. She leaned forward. Then he raised his arms, dissolving into her upturned face.

*It is in such silences that we lose our sanity*, Jay knew too well. He had looked up and seen only the stricken look on Siti's face. Confused, he had turned to the shadows, then back to the TV, oblivious.

Siti had drawn on her *semangat* and willed Shanti to die. The curse of a mother is powerful, and Shanti had been cursed by two. How could she have survived that?

Shapna, too, went berserk when she heard about the pregnancy.

"His bastard child!" she shrieked, putting Shanti's hand on her own head. "Swear on me you will have nothing to do with him again."

Shanti steeled herself. "I cannot swear on your life," she said, while Shapna screamed, "Slut! You will never become a Fatimah or Aishah or whatever the hell it is you want, with your bastard child. You might as well kill yourself now; it will be the same thing!"

Jay remained silent through it all.

# Nineteen

Agni's voice broke the silence. "And then? What about Zainal and my mother? They wanted to marry each other, right? *Tarpor?*"

*Was this the time to tell her the truth?* Agni's voice brought Jay back to the open air hawker stalls functioning as a huge food court under balmy skies, fragrant with mingling cuisines. He heard the shouts of the clients with the languages all mixed up; names of foods learnt from the languages of the hawkers, never translated, and even he had once known how to order exactly what he wanted in Cantonese, Hokkien, or Hakka. The words hadn't fazed him at all, all these cultures comingling in a history that was older than anyone alive. He looked at Agni and thought, not just yet.

"My father," he cleared his throat and kept his voice even, "well, he tried to talk to Zainal. But Zainal frowned when he emerged from the shadows of the jacaranda tree, and sneered about my father lecturing about *illicit liaisons*. He, Zainal, had not pursued a married woman and, since his religion allowed more than one wife, he was willing to marry Shanti. Something like that."

"And then?"

"Zainal, I remember, called him a *Pendatang. Pendatang* as in the newly arrived. The immigrant. The one who had no –"

"I know what it means," said Agni, irritated. "*Tarpor?*"

"Your grandmother said Siti put up a hate charm, murmuring, '*Umamman Chan Ta-man Chan*' seven times in a single breath and blowing on slaked lime, then marking their fence so that the hatred would take firm hold."

Agni moved her plate to the side brusquely. "And that was that? A magic charm, your father insulted, and everyone gave up?"

"They had to. Siti and Zainal disappeared that night, never to return again. Just as everyone knew they would." They both remained silent for some time. "Maybe Shanti thought the child would force their hand, but this one tore everyone apart."

"It's me, Professor," Agni snapped. "That child is *me*."

"Yes. Well, she did want you. She wouldn't consider any other solution, and they tried... well, you can imagine. She really wanted a daughter – only a daughter – Agnibina. Do you know what it means?" From the recesses of his memory, Jay dredged up a long-forgotten tune and softly sang the lines of a Bengali song:

> *What melodies play in your lute of Fire?*
> *The heavens tremble with the stars aflame,*
> *Inebriated by your song.*

Agni smiled ruefully, "Music that ignites the soul, that's me."

"She wanted you to change the world."

"Not just change, but fire it up, Professor," Agni said archly, "although fires can be quite traumatic, eh?"

He looked away. "Why do you say that?"

Agni picked up a napkin, delicately dabbing at her lips. "Well... anyway, let it go. I am grateful to you for being in the fire, and for Zainal rescuing you so that he would eventually meet my mother and I would be born. Despite everything that happened, I think you did *me* a favour by getting lost in that fire."

"Hang on!" Jay was laughing, pleasantly surprised to realise that his hands weren't betraying his nervous memories right now, "I'm not sure I want to take any credit. I ended up as a pawn in that story when all I really wanted was the Queen!"

Agni cocked her head at him, and Jay realised what he had just said. He picked up his *teh tarik* to sip the last of the milky tea.

That was when the Malay stall keeper appeared. Without a word, he picked up the fork and spoon on Jay's plate and flung them into a nearby drain.

"What the hell is going on?" Jay got up so quickly that the red plastic chair he had been sitting on crashed to the ground.

The Malay man started to shout.

"What is he saying?" Jay turned to Agni.

"Something about the forks and spoons from the Malay and Chinese stalls getting mixed up and contaminated." Agni whispered hurriedly.

"Contaminated? By what?"

By this time, a crowd had collected, and other hawkers started discussing the problem in loud Malay. Jay could hear the word *haram* being repeated. He looked at the Chinese hawkers for help, but two of them just stood by the sidelines, one softly scratching an arm and the other watching intently.

"But we didn't order any pork, Uncle!" Agni tried reasoning in English and switched to Malay even as the stall keeper grew livid beyond reason. Jay opened his wallet and took out a couple of notes, waving them uncertainly in the air.

The Malay hawker didn't want money, he shouted; who did they think they were? Jay began to feel the eyes of the mob grow hostile, and the heat pouring down through the serrated tin roof felt like molten metal on his skin. Just the fact that Jay's cutlery may have been near pork, the most *haram* of all, was enough. There was nothing left to argue about.

Jay remembered the CNN footage on the street riots in Kuala Lumpur just a couple of days ago, and felt slightly dizzy. What could he do if this group got really ugly?

"Let's go," said Agni angrily. She gathered her jacket and pulled on Jay's arm, hurriedly throwing some notes on the table. She didn't look back. Jay, both confused and furious in that hostile crowd of people whom he barely understood, hurried to follow her lead, stumbling on the fallen chair.

They didn't stop until they had reached Old Coliseum Café. Then Agni squeezed Jay's arm in sympathy. "Look, I'm sorry.

This is not normal. I think the unrest in the streets is making everyone edgy a bit —"

He pulled away. "Edgy? Why? Is it because I'm American? Did that fellow just pick a fight because of my accent?"

"Why would you think that?" asked Agni. "Sometimes Indian men pick fights if they see an Indian woman with a foreigner, but I don't think that the 'uncle' back there had any such motive."

Jay realised that she was trying to lighten the atmosphere, but he was still fuming inside. "Well, something set him off, and I don't think it was the fork or the effing spoon!"

He had stopped abruptly in the middle of the road. Agni grasped his gesticulating hand firmly and said, "They are not all jihadis, Prof."

Jay took a deep breath. She was right. "Okay. But that bastard was really frothing at the mouth... Geez!"

"Yes. I'm sorry," Agni's voice sounded timid.

Jay raised an awkward arm towards her shoulder and withdrew quickly as Agni stepped back, startled. "Oops, I wouldn't want one of your Malaysian-Indian brothers to come raging down the warpath now!"

At Leboh Ampang, where the air was heavy with the smell of *sambar* and sandalwood incense, they ducked into a narrow alleyway that led to the parking garage. In between the tailors and the newspaper vendors, a Chinese fortune-teller called out loudly, "Sir! Try your fortune – five ringgit only! Guaranteed hundred per cent accurate."

"One minute, Agni." Jay drew her into the stall by splaying his fingers on the small of her back, and lightly pushing her in. "I remember this!" He tossed the coins up like a child, flicking the large golden balls that twirled in the air, then sank to reveal lines drawn in heads and tails. Agni laughed at his excitement as the sixth line formed and the entire image was revealed.

"Very auspicious," said the fortune-teller. "The upper trigram, here, it is Chên — takes the situation out of danger. The danger is in the lower trigram, which is the Abysmal, Water. This is the beginning of the end of trouble."

Jay looked at Agni, and they burst into laughter. Jay handed over the fee, with a generous tip.

"Thank you!" the fortune-teller beamed, "and here is a souvenir for you." He handed Jay a small scroll, rolled up like parchment.

Inside was a poem.

> *The thunder rolls Deliverance*
> *If there is no call for action*
> *Return brings good fortune*
> *If action is called for*
> *Hastening brings good fortune*

Jay looked delighted. "I like it!" he said.

Agni mocked him gently. "And just when I thought you might be more Charles Bukowski than Khalil Gibran, Professor."

Jay folded the poem, and put it carefully in his pocket. "I think it's time you stopped calling me, Professor, don't you?"

Agni looked at her watch. "I was supposed to be at the airport fifteen minutes ago. Shall we go?"

## Twenty

Colonel S looked out of the windows of the reclaimed factory in Nilai. The immense stretch of concrete lay desolate except for his lone car and the guard's small motorcycle.

Again, he regretted his lack of attention to a small detail – the fact that Jay's cellphone did not roam in Malaysia. And Jay was refusing a local SIM. Which left Jay unreachable for long hours, to roam like an unyoked cow, instead of doing the job he had been brought here to do. But Colonel S could not push Jay too far, too soon; he needed to save his energy for bigger battles.

Colonel S punched the keys on the computer, getting into Jay's personal files, and searching for something he could use.

He briefly wondered what this girl now looked like, that granddaughter of Shapna's. Colonel S had severed all connections with that family the night Zainal and Siti disappeared. Shapna had been a whore, had brought up Shanti to be a whore, and Colonel S had no doubt that the granddaughter would also be an easy lay for Jay. Unfortunately, he couldn't wait for Jay to tire of this girl.

Sluts were so common in this country. Women who were never taught to cover their bodies and pray five times a day, washing themselves and their minds with a habitual holy ritual... there were too many migrant breeds. More kept coming in, like that Tibetan girl. Promiscuity spilled over to politics, and then it became a national problem, when the cure was basic modesty as explained in the Holy Book. Why was that so hard to implement?

Not that all Malays would agree with him on this. When Siti's daughters were growing up, Colonel S remembered the new way of Islamic dressing, the *fesyen dakwah*, as an extremist joke, something that Muslim parents like Zainal and Siti would smile about. *Aiyah, don't know which is worse, lah, having my daughter return in a miniskirt, or a tudung!*

Colonel S had never married. Zainal's family had filled his own life. Despite everyone's urging, he had never found a woman pious enough to marry for life. Women, he decided early on, were an unnecessary complication, leading men to indiscretions beyond their control.

If left to the mini-dressed Chinese and belly-baring Indian women, the men in this country would all be as castrated as that Jay Ghosh and his whoring father. This country was still full of pious Muslims because the women of the *ummah* were the backbone of this country, and Colonel S would always be thankful for that. Which was why killing a Malay woman was something he had trouble doing. Killing any woman was hard, and he still thought of that Tibetan woman, especially her incandescent beauty on that moonlit night. But killing his first Malay woman had been harder, breaking her neck and throwing her into the swampy marshes... and he had been so young.

He scrolled through the data detailing Jay's work in designing and modifying polymers for biomedical applications. Jay's work was closely associated with local hospitals, and included the prestigious National Heart Centre as well as a well-known cancer centre.

His prodigy had done well for himself; Colonel S allowed himself a measure of self-congratulation. Jay had been a miserable child, abandoned at that fire in an amusement park and left to die, then abandoned through his teenage years with a distraught mother for company while his father fucked Shapna. Jay's mother, Ila, was a strong woman, no doubt about that. There were no tantrums, no embarrassing signs of trauma, and she was always there for her two sons. When her children went on stage at school plays, she was always in the audience, and stood behind the *rosogolla* stall at the Deepavali fundraiser, smiling, with only her children by her side.

Jay had learnt well from her. To hold his anger close to his heart, and to never let that howl escape. But Colonel S had seen the trauma, and mentored Jay into a position of prominence in Seattle. Colonel S had done all this, even after Jay's father, like so many foreigners, had chosen to abandon Malaysia and emigrate elsewhere.

He didn't fully understand the responsibility he felt for Jay, and Jay did not treat Colonel S with the godlike respect that Colonel S had for Zainal. If you saved a child, over and over again, did he become so much your own that you forgave his shortcomings?

All this was a small matter in the greater scheme of things. Jay was brilliant in his science, so what if he was emotionally crippled? He probably could not love anyone in any way after what had happened with Shanti. Colonel S just needed Jay's unflinching loyalty.

He flipped through the sections describing new work with the biodegradable polymers, the injectable implants and nanoparticles, all leading to more effective gene and drug delivery. His own work was nowhere near as reconstructive. It was as if he and Jay now stood at opposite sides of the same spectrum, using the same technology for very different ends.

Jay's work in developing and testing fully biodegradable stent technology would be the most applicable for the cause. The mechanical integrity would last for as long as three or four weeks – giving them the gift of enough time. The properties of cellular-friendly polymer had reduced scarring too. Warriors around the world suffered due to the limits of thermoplasticity in their present method, but Jay's expertise would solve a lot of the problems.

He shuffled through a folder quickly to find a timeline on the sheet of paper. He would have to move fast to cover his tracks, but he would do it. The two bodyguards were in jail for the death of the Tibetan model, but the online bloggers were sniffing at his heels. Colonel S would need to intelligently manoeuvre the balance of blame and patriotism that the present plan required.

The muezzin's call from a nearby mosque reminded him it was time to go.

It was a pity that Jay was turning out to be just like his whore-worshipping father... It was a good thing that he, Colonel S, knew how to control such men. He already had a lifetime of practice from holding the balls of all the adulterous Malaysian politicians he dealt with on a daily basis.

# Twenty-one

Abhik glanced at the clock on the dashboard as the sudden rain started raking fingers of water down his windscreen. His meeting with the Sisters in Islam had taken longer than he had anticipated, and he would be late unless he drove faster.

The radio blared *Theocracy or Democracy? The burning issues today... Welcome to our discussion for the evening and in the studio today we have...*

The Hindsight 2020 campaign was such a fuck-up. The leaders were determined to march on the streets again, campaigning for minority rights but, as police permission for such a gathering would not ever be granted, Abhik would have to bail out people again. The Prime Minister had personally signed the order for the five ringleaders to be indefinitely detained. The Hindsight 2020 leader who had fled to London to petition the British Government was not making any headway.

It was too chaotic. He only hoped that there would be no bloodshed but, with the accusations of discrimination and marginalisation flying back and forth in the media, he could hear the increasing stridency on both sides.

*Happy Deepavali!* He brutally cut off the chirpy advertisement on the radio. No one else seemed to care about anything important in this country.

There was so much going on in Malaysia that Agni should be a part of, but if she chose to spend all her time escorting older American men around town, there was not a damn thing that he could do about it.

Yet he and Agni had been taught the same brand of patriotism in the same school. All the Malaysians at the international school were headed for an overseas education; having choices in this country was only for the rich. Yet, how encompassing the words of the Malaysian national anthem sounded:

*Negaraku, tanah tumpahnya darahku*
*Rakyat hidup bersatu dan maju*
*My country, the land where my blood flows*
*Citizens live united and progressive*

When the fifth grade teacher, Mrs Narayanan, had taught them the words in school, she got misty-eyed and talked about the womb-blood of the newborn falling onto the ground and becoming one with the country, tying the infant forever to the land of its birth.

"Cock," Abhik had sniffed in an undertone, already a rebel at eleven. "Someone should tell her to stop watching the stupid Tamil movies that fill her head with such rubbish."

He had put up his hand and challenged Mrs Narayanan. "How about the immigrants then? Whose womb-blood fell in another country?"

Mrs Narayanan heaved her ample bosom and replied, "When a man leaves his home to toil in another, his sweat and tears fall and mingle into the new earth, which then adopts him to give him a new motherland."

"She's completely *gila*," Abhik had loudly whispered, one finger corkscrewing his right temple for added effect.

He had always been so certain that his future lay outside Malaysia. But Agni bought into the image of blood emerging from the umbilical cord to mingle with the land, creating a bond stronger than any other. When he and Agni both left, urged by their relatives to seek a more level playing field on foreign shores, they both came reeling back.

Abhik knew he wanted this imperfect existence on a congenial soil, where the sarong *kebaya* and the *sari*, the gaudy and the plain, were perfectly interchangeable. He loved the *Rojak* salad of the land, the crisp green cucumber as distinct as the rubbery squid, the whiteness of the egg a contrast to the crush of the peanut, all sweet and sour and hot and pungent, all mixed up together in a clash of the senses.

This land was like no other. There could be no substitute for this cacophonous warp and weft of dissimilarity that sparkled in the brilliant sunshine. There was so much interbreeding in the country's history that Malaysia now sold its *Truly Asia* charms in glossy brochures; this orgiastic spawning of the Indian, Chinese, and Malay races had occurred because sex knew no boundaries – Agni was proof of that. In Malaysia, how could one begin to distinguish the pure Malay 'sons of the soil' from the mongrel breed?

His phone buzzed, and over the speaker he could hear the familiar voice:

"Confirm already, client in the office in two hours. Where the fuck are you?"

The client didn't come in the next two hours; he made them wait for six. Abhik waited with the elderly Punjabi lawyer and one of the clerical staff, the three of them sitting in the meeting room, each one silently counting the many ways things could have gone wrong.

The Punjabi lawyer, a senior partner at the firm, was in a wheelchair. His white hair was hidden under a navy-blue turban, but his lush white beard barely hid the wrinkled mouth that had shouted for human rights in Malaysia for nearly six decades of an illustrious career. The Punjabi lawyer now represented the Tibetan model's family in the Malaysian courts. As the murdered woman's father roamed the halls of the Malaysian justice system, this lion-lawyer gave him the only glimmer of hope.

Not that the lionisation was easy, even in old age. Last month, he had been surrounded by a heckling group of young Malay political wannabes and he could not steer himself out of their enraged mass. All because he had made a reference to a popular Bollywood movie to express his commitment to winning – *Singh is Kinng* – and the youths had seized on the phrase as an insult to the Malay monarchy.

This lawyer had fought back – but he was getting old, and tired. Abhik saw his head slump gently forward as a soft snore escaped his pursed lips.

There was the click of a door opening, and the client walked in. The elderly lawyer's eyes were wide open again as Abhik looked at his watch; it was eighteen minutes past ten at night.

"Mr Singh. Abhik. Thank you for waiting."

The meeting room was lit by a single hanging lamp and resembled a police interrogation room. None of the men in the room made a move to switch on more lights as they settled into their chairs.

The client had baggy circles under his eyes, and sported stubble marked by uneven greyness. He was a well-known blogger and a respected academic, as well as a government critic. The royal blood flowing in his veins made his anti-government messages an easy target for charges of envy; the princeling's wife was this man's first cousin.

He gratefully extended a hand for the coffee and then stared into its murky depths. Abhik noted how dishevelled this usually well-groomed aristocrat looked today, his shirt so crumpled that it appeared he had slept in it.

Singh cleared his throat. "Thank you for coming... This will mean a lot to my client's case, but I hope you fully understand the danger to yourself."

The client smiled. "Let's get started, shall we?"

The statutory declaration was laid out on the table painstakingly by the elderly lawyer. Abhik thought he detected a shake in the gnarled fingers as he skimmed over the words again, those lines implicating the princeling and his wife. Now on the table for everyone to see in black and white were the words:

*My informer states that Colonel S was the person who placed
the C4 on various parts of the victim's body witnessed by...
I make this statutory declaration because I have been reliably
informed about the involvement of these three people who have
thus far not been implicated in the murder, nor called as
witnesses by the prosecution in the ongoing trial at the Shah
Alam High Court.
I also make this statutory declaration because I am aware that it
is a crime not to reveal evidence that may help the police in its
investigation of the crime.*

The client picked up the Montblanc pen on the table and signed with a deep indentation.

Singh picked up the papers and scrutinised them again, rustling the two pages.

"You say here that you have been 'reliably informed that a senior minister has received a written report from military intelligence confirming what you have revealed'. Are you sure you want to say this?"

The client frowned. "Yes. And, before you ask me again, yes also to the statement that one of the rulers has been briefed about this matter. I know this... all of it."

"You will be detained under the ISA," said Abhik.

Both men turned to him in irritation. "I know, young man, but it won't be my first time," replied the client. "This is my country, and I can say this because of who I am. Therefore I must."

"Our country," Singh corrected him gently, "but you are right; very few people can speak up as you have been doing."

The client acknowledged the barb with a slight nod. "You are preaching to the converted my friend; I, too, want One Malaysia for all Malaysians." He turned to Abhik, "I need to go. Can I leave you to finish this, or do you need me here?"

Singh nodded at Abhik before clasping the client's right hand in a firm handshake. "Thank you again. This will make a big difference. And rock some political sampans."

"I only want that murderer to rot in hell, Mr Singh. No political ambitions here, only nationalism. They may say what they like on the streets, but I don't ever want to hear this implication from you again."

Abhik collected the sheaf of papers in his hand and reached for the clear folder. A collage of pictures stared back at him: the young Tibetan model in a shampoo advertisement, her black hair gleaming against the white orchids tucked behind her ear and smiling so hard that her eyes crinkled with delight; then the picture of a barren field, burnt into black patches with bloody body parts; then the close up of a black silk scarf, thrown to the ground in the shape of batwings.

Abhik angrily shoved the papers into the folder, obscuring the photographs completely. He heard the soft swish of the door closing behind the client and Singh, as he registered their murmured goodbyes.

## Twenty-two

If only all older men were equally harmless.

Abhik had called and, for the first time in this relationship, Agni heard a hint of possessiveness. "Bondhu!" he fumed, "It's impossible to get anything but voicemail when you're out spending time with the American *dadu* again."

"Give me a break, Abhik! He's a *dadu* alright, old enough to be my father!"

"With your track record, B, being old enough to be your father *is* the big attraction."

She hadn't thought about this possibility earlier. Certainly not when she had dropped Jay off at Chinatown, pointed him towards the Moorish colonnades of the railway station and the national mosque, told him that they used to be the most photographed buildings in Malaysia before the Petronas Towers, and driven off towards the airport. Since then, she had been preoccupied with the airport problems, and had focused all her energy on work.

Now, manoeuvring through the narrow labyrinths of the back offices at the airport, Agni reflected that maybe Jay liked her company a little too much. That *almost* hug near Leboh Ampang had been unnerving. Older Bengali men did not behave like that. She wasn't looking for a relationship with another man old enough to be her father. Definitely not another American. Abhik and she were still trying to understand what was happening between them and, although it seemed so nebulous, it was enough for her. For now.

She should tell Jay about Abhik. She had hinted at it earlier, but maybe it was time to make it clear. She may be misinterpreting any interest; the man seemed half-crazed about her mother. What was with the pendant around his neck he kept touching when he spoke about her? The guy could barely keep his hands still at any time! Next time, she should just ask him outright whether that had belonged to her mother, mention Abhik as a casual note in her own romantic history, and let it drop.

She stopped at the satellite building of the airport, and peered into the darkness of the car park. This was where she had met Greg, six years ago.

The airport project brought Greg to Asia, where his team was hired by the Malaysian government to ensure the new airport would be "World Class," whatever that meant. Greg, who had flown to Malaysia to forget a bitter divorce, had seen Agni on the lacerated soil of the airport site on a hot tropical afternoon.

"You were my mirage, Hon'," he said later. "Such a hot day and there you were, shimmering, in oasis-blue silk, the heat making the air behind you waver. I didn't stand a chance darlin'!"

Weeks later, while snuggling up against each other during a long lunch break in his apartment, he would tell her that the secretaries had already told him that Agni was "itchy," but the innocuous Malay word *gatal* contained a multitude of meanings. "*Just fixin' this itch,*" he would drawl, scratching her inner thighs with his stubble.

His condominium was next to the office, and their long lunch breaks made them both lose weight. More than the expatriate lifestyle he offered, it was his old-world gallantry Agni found irresistible. She was a young engineer on her first multinational project, and Greg provided the first glimpse into a more glamorous lifestyle. Agni had lost her virginity to an aging rock musician who had wooed her with his ballads, but that relationship had flagged against the relentless consumerism of Kuala Lumpur.

She knew enough to indulge Greg; once the project was over, he was sure to leave. In the meantime, she found him a heady experience, a growing-up addiction.

She liked the way he asked for what he wanted, and got it. She loved the way he touched her. Greg would lift her wrist, kissing the vein that throbbed inside, his tongue darting in delightful circles. "You have such fine bones," he once said, circling her wrist with thumb and forefinger and twisting lightly.

"Compared to yours?" She teased. "It's all the dead meat you eat. Pretty soon you *matsallehs* all start looking like dead beefy slabs, yah?"

She ducked from his pillow.

"Don't knock my diet, woman," Greg mock-growled. "I once lassoed a fridge with a chain and hoisted it on my back when I was moving apartments. Couldn't get all that strength from the fart-food you eat."

Greg's appetite was a revelation in many ways. He had prowled the cities of Asia, tasting its women like samples on a buffet. "Hon'," he teased Agni one day, "such a smorgasbord, amazing women of all sizes!"

The Malaysian airport project was a hothouse of liaisons, mostly illicit. The women were largely local clerical staff, even the young Malay woman who surprised them all with her fluent German. The Australians, the Swedes, the Welsh, and the Norwegians, none of the men were exempt from a furtive grope in the car park, in elevators, in places hidden from their wives who sipped afternoon margaritas while the children were cared for by Filipino maids.

Was it the brevity of an engineering project that encouraged this suspension of morality? The men would complain about bureaucratic corruption, accepting as their due the perks of colluding with the powerful. Screwing the local women was a perk too. Sure, they reasoned, working closely together with their assistants until two or three in the morning to meet project milestones led to temptations that were hard to resist. It was easy for both parties, this quick fuck on a non-negotiable deadline.

That's what Agni had thought too.

But when the project was winding up, Greg reeled her in. He spoke of a university in the town he was returning to, no racial quotas to keep her out, just a mingling of the best brains and thoughts. Agni ended up in a small college town in Texas for two years, ostensibly studying for a Master's in Computer Science. She did not tell her grandmother about Greg.

It wasn't that bad actually, small-town Texas; the worst was becoming Agnes from Agni, but at least her surname didn't change. They never did marry, although the issue hung between them like a problem easily rectified, like halitosis or some problem with a fancy medical name and a traditional cure.

Using Greg to get her degree was something Agni did with a clean conscience. Sex with him was fun, and she was innovative enough to make him feel he was getting his dose of *kama sutra*, as advertised. She was his bit of exotica that made fragrant *pilau* as a side dish when his colleagues served grilled trout, and she had once whipped up an ethnic *tandoori* turkey for a Thanksgiving with a difference. She never intended anything to be permanent, but being his hothouse orchid in the field of magnolias started to take its toll.

"Oh, Agnes!" A guest would shriek, helping herself to more *pilau*, "I *love* Indian food!"

"But we don't eat none of that, sweetie," she would continue, pointing to the curry. "Goats are pets where I come from."

Ultimately, it wasn't the food that made Agni realise how foreign she was; it was the colour of turmeric.

She cooked through her homesickness, conjuring up what she had left behind by being able to close her eyes and smell and taste. Her favourite dishes out of her grandmother's Malaysian kitchen all had the yellow paste melded into the flavour. As she made those dishes in her Texan kitchen, Agni would relentlessly cover her tracks, mopping up the obstinate yellow splatters before they became a part of the spotless laminates. She scrubbed with abrasives, detergents, and bleach, yet the yellow stains on the tabletop, the blender, the kitchen towel, the microwave oven, and her nails – all of it would be a fresh reproach when the sunshine poured in every morning. A gaudy colour, so out of place.

She knew how superficial this sounded. She knew because she had tried to explain it to her friend, Nisha, and found herself stuttering over the inanity of what she was saying. During that time, when her relationship with Greg was unravelling and finding someone to talk to was almost impossible, Nisha had become her rock.

Unfortunately, Nisha could barely sit up straight, she was laughing so hard. "Agni, it's a yellow *stain*. Even if you had to constantly get it out, you could. It must be, um, the sex, right?"

"No!" she tried again, "Okay, you know, last Saraswati Puja, when I had to find a yellow *sari* to wear? And he just didn't understand? I turned all the closets inside out, and I had to find a yellow *sari*, and he said, '*Hon' you'd look lovely in this blue...*'"

Nisha rolled her eyes. "So? I don't get it either; it's a Bengali thing! Agni, *you* have a problem with yellow."

"Ha, ha, Nish."

Nisha drained the orange juice, and then slowly tore off little white pillows from her styrofoam cup, squelching them between thumb and forefinger. "What are you looking for, Agni? So many excuses," she paused thoughtfully, "do you just want a fuckbuddy?"

"Huh?"

Nisha cocked her head slightly. "Maybe it's everyone calling you Agnes all the time. Get off it, Agni, this is not a colour problem."

She *knew* it wasn't just her name being mangled, although

that did bother her. But she considered herself lucky. Her male Malaysian friend with the common Chinese name of Ng, an impossible sound for the Texans to replicate, became 'Angie' in the land of JRs and Dubyas. They became pals, Angie and Agnes, the misnomers whose names were so easily interchangeable.

She ended the relationship after two years in Texas, after her old boss called her to see if she was interested in a job in Singapore. She left Greg in Houston, both of them agreeing that it was time to put some space between them.

Within three months, Greg was in Singapore for a conference at Suntec City. He said, *"No strings attached, Hon'. I need a holiday. I'll stay at a hotel."*

Of course he didn't. He dropped his bags in her Zen-minimalist loft off Maxwell Road, and kissed her. After that, it was so easy to fall into bed together, no initial awkwardness despite their months apart, halting small talk taking them from a hesitant *might not happen* to a mood charged with inevitability. His jaw was rough with the stubble she liked, and the roughness merged with the moistness of his lips grazing her neck. She sank into his smell, aftershave mingling into sweat from the tropical heat. He teased a soft nibbling path across her belly, gently sucking her skin while his hands roamed her thighs.

A practiced seduction, comforting in its familiarity. When they came together, perfectly tight, she was a winged Pegasus exploding towards the sun.

They lay coiled and speechless for a while, both taken aback by how easily they had reached for each other. Then Greg said, *Come back with me*, and she laughed. They went downstairs to eat at one of the fusion cafés dotting the pastel-coloured row of restored historical shophouses. Greg's two weeks in Singapore stretched into three.*Come back with me*, he said again and again.

Greg was so stable, so comforting... so *dull*. Singapore was filled with older Caucasian men with young Sarong Party Girls, those exotic Asian pieces so fuckable and forgettable. Agni recognised the derisive looks directed at her as she strolled hand in hand with Greg through the esplanade. Being one of those wild and wanton amoral young things whom Greg was throwing cash and trinkets at would have been preferable, for it was depressing being in this staid relationship with a man so tenacious that he was impossible to shake off.

Agni knew she had been warped by her mother and her grandmother. Her mother had died for love, and her grandmother had broken social norms to become the mistress of a married man. She wanted a relationship that was like a phoenix rising, giving up everything for love. But, instead of being a spectacular, incendiary winged bird, Greg was a rather cool penguin, both feet on the ground.

The bright lights of the highway told Agni it was time to go home. Tomorrow was the big party at Abhik's, and she needed sleep to handle both Jay and Abhik in the same room. Especially if Abhik was getting testy. She couldn't blame him, with all the Hindsight protestors and the Tibetan woman's case giving him a double dose of stress every single day.

She also needed to find out why her grandmother hated Professor Jay Ghosh so much. But, for now, she just needed to call Abhik and tell him it was too late to see him tonight; that she was going straight home.

# Twenty-three

*The front grill is jangling; I can hear Agni wrestling with the three locks and I hear her swearing softly, but there is no one to help. Zu is asleep already, as is the night nurse, gently snoring on the armchair by my bed. That is all they are good for, the hired help, sleeping the sleep of the dead.*

*But sleep does not come to me. I stay awake, praying for the child to reach safely home. I wait for Agni to return, even on the nights that stretch till dawn. I can hear the door creaking open, and now, the double locking click on the grill on the front door.*

*She should have a man by her who would keep her safe in this darkness. Then, sleep would come easier to me, especially now that Jayanta has come back. It was such a shock to see him – after so many years – and so whole and healthy. He was such an emotional cripple, unable to stop his circling hands, his stuttering... I expected him to be grotesque, hunchbacked by his wants.*

*I fear for my Agni. Young women are blown up in fields near the old airport and no one is hanged for it. The case goes unresolved from court to court. What hope is there for people like us when someone as evil as Jay returns?*

*Agni is peering into the bedroom, so I invite her in with a soft sound. "You should be asleep, Dida! It's been such a long day," she scolds me, but her tone is tender as she snuggles up to me, taking care not to roll over my outflung arm in the dark.*

*I smell the smoke in my granddaughter's hair, but I breathe in deeply anyway, just stroking her hair in ragged lines.*

*There are too many secrets between us.*

*She murmurs sleepily, stifling a yawn. "I am so knocked out Dida." She kisses my forehead. "You need to stop staying up for me every time."*

*I grunt, and she touches my face softly.*

*"Try to get some sleep, okay?"*

*Then the door closes and she is gone.*

*There is the buzzing sound of a telephone and Agni's full-throated laughter floats into the room, riding on a night breeze that is heavy with the fragrant quisqualis flowers unfurling pink and white. I had so little to laugh about at her age. I was already a wife and a mistress, with the burden of two men and a young child.*

*I wonder if Jay has called again, and pray that she is not laughing that laugh for him.*

*Jay called here this morning. He told the idiot nurse that he had lost Agni's office number and she gave it to him, saying the number wrong the first time. I made a lot of noise, trying to distract her, but she just turned her back on me, put a hand over her ear and gave him Agni's office and mobile numbers, looking them up on her mobile phone. I have to get rid of this nurse; she is stupid, and impertinent too. She treats me like a willful child she hates.*

*Then he called again, asking for Mridula's number. The nurse chattily told me he was invited to the Open House tomorrow. I know why he is calling so many times. He wants me to know that he is after something. He wants me to spend sleepless nights, like this, worrying about what he is doing with my granddaughter.*

*He looks at her as if he is searching for something, but there is lust in his eyes. He has his father's eyes; I know that look too well.*

*If he was obsessed with Shanti – maybe he still is – he should leave Agni alone. Perhaps his obsession has festered into an unnatural hunger… I see it so clearly. An open-mouthed greed. I hope Agni can see it too. Desires should not grow so monstrous.*

*True strength is in resisting your desires, instead of succumbing to them. Falling in love is such an absurdity, with such predictable endings. Initially, the sustaining interest – that delicious unwrapping of the folds that make up another person. But when the layers are uncovered to the pulsating heart beneath, to its nakedness and imperfections, what mystery is left? Everything changes and you*

*realise that love is just shadow play and, like the immense shadows*
*of a wayang kulit, it too is soon folded away.*

*Lust I understand. The body's ache, a hollow core empty for*
*another, any other – that is real; that is true.*

*I wish I had known this Malay story before my marriage to*
*Nikhil. But this ancient story was never a part of my childhood, so I*
*didn't know it until much later. And then, it was too late to tell my*
*daughter that a prince should not always get what he wants,*
*especially an aged prince:*

*Sultan Mahmud's wife passed away and he grieved deeply.*
*He decided he needed an extraordinary woman to ease his pain,*
*someone skilled and beautiful, like the princess of Gunung*
*Ledang, who lived on a high mountain in Johor.*
*Sultan Mahmud sent his nobles to the enchanted mountain,*
*and the strong winds blew hard and the rains pelted the men,*
*shielding the mountain with dark clouds.*
*Finally, after days of much hardship, they came to a garden.*
*The brooks bubbled merrily over the stones and the birds of*
*redyellowgreen flitted from the branches.*
*In the middle of the garden was a wonderful gazebo. It was made*
*of human bones, with a roof of human hair. Inside this strange*
*structure sat an old lady with her handmaidens.*
*The lady asked, "What brings you here, noble sirs, so far from*
*your own kingdom?"*
*"We wish to convey the sultan's wishes to the princess," said the*
*men, and related their story.*
*The old woman listened. Then she disappeared for a short while.*
*When she returned, she said to the nobles:*
*"The Princess of Mount Ledang has heard all that you have said.*
*Now please tell the Sultan that this is what the Princess has to*
*say: The Princess agrees to marry him, but with the following*
*conditions. As dowry, he is to provide:*

*A gold bridge and a silver bridge from Malacca to Gunung Ledang*

*Seven trays of the heart of mosquitoes*

*Seven dishes of louse livers*

*A jar of women's tears*

*A jar of young areca nut juice*

*A bowl of the Sultan's own blood*

*And*

*A bowl of the blood of the young crown prince, Raja Ahmad.*

*Only then will the princess accept the Sultan of Melaka's proposal of marriage."*

*When the Sultan heard all this, he was quiet for a long time.*

*"She can have all she asks for," he said, "except for the blood of my son."*

*And the marriage plans were cancelled.*

*A son's pain on one side; on the other, lust fulfilled. Nikhil made the trade because my exultant heart had leapt up and said: Yes, I will, yes, yes, yes!*

*Nikhil brought me to Malaya. I was fifteen when I met my husband.*

*When Nikhil came for the bride-viewing in 1931, he was a civil servant in Calcutta, at a time when the British were the real gods. He was also a sometimes-poet, a fashionable accomplishment for such times, which made him not unlike the thousands of other Bengali gentlemen who wanted to be Tagore.*

*If I close my eyes I can still see our courtyard in Calcutta, heavy Doric columns flanking a red-cemented courtyard, filled with buzzing flies and hurrying people. There was the hum of bustling servants bearing Ilish dripping blood in fresh slaughter, plucked from the Ganges waters to be cooked with stinging mustard and chillies. Then the Koi fish, struggling for life, beaten on the head with vicious scythes but writhing fitfully, refusing to breathe their* defeat. I was brought up hearing that a woman's life is like that of a Koi fish, hanging on to life, despite all odds.

Such was the idiom of acceptance for other women; never for me.

For I was young and in full bloom. I could not but know of this power, although no one would tell me so. But the sooty kajol they applied under my hairline, and on my cheek to distract the evil eye, told me about this visitation of divine grace on a body I rarely had occasion to think about. How quickly I learnt to recognise that indrawn breath, that attempt at nonchalance! And how I revelled in it!

My father, like most gentlemen who frequented our house, had more learning than wealth. Delighted at my birth, he gave me the outrageous name of Shapnasundari, Beautiful-As-A-Dream. How could I not fulfill his prophecy, accept his benediction, at least for a few brief years? So I had willpower, and I had the gift of beauty. I practiced using them both. I was sure I could bend destiny to my will.

At fifteen I was ripe for marriage. A suitable boy had been found, and that is why I glowed as the courtyard hummed on that morning, buzzing with activity for me.

It was just before the puja season, as the breezes cooled and wafted heavy with the incense of the shefali and bokul flowers, and I remember a baul singing outside my window, dressed in ochre robes and strumming the ektara.

I have always loved music but, more than anything else, I loved reading about history. I spent days escaping from the monsoon into empires and wars, the treacherous and the heroic. Cramped into the small space between a Burmese teak four-poster and the damp wall, with the mould seeping into my splayed toes, I hid from prying eyes and read of magical Malaya through the dim light seeping through dark-grey clouds. It was Malaya then; this country became Malaysia later.

I first found Malaya in a Bengali poem about the sea maiden lover of an Indian voyager. It was a land whose cities rolled off my tongue with the flavours of the fabulous: Kedah, Perak, Malacca. Walking in the garden, I whispered the name of Sungei Bujang that swooped into the estuary of Merbok, where a bronze image of a Buddha from the fifth century was found. I traced my fingers over a print of this relic from the early Hindu colonisation of Kedah. The plump bronze Buddha always smiled his benediction, one arm outstretched, one hip slightly exaggerated in its bend, the other arm grasping something between thumb and forefinger. I imagined the curly hair in round Grecian clumps, the metal smoothed by the ravages of time.

But first, there was the bride-viewing.

When the groom's party invaded our courtyard, accepting deference as their due and marching into our home as regally as only such a large party could, I was enjoying the attention being showered on me. Mani was very distracted, arranging the folds of my sari and tucking a loose tendril of hair affectionately behind my ear, her eyes wet with tears.

Then Mani ran out to welcome the groom's delegation. The groom-to-be, a shy plump boy, lagged behind the men of the groom's family who stared boldly around them with assessing eyes.

Mani had taught me to look directly at the world; my gaze did not scuttle around the periphery of faces as it should have, but held the male gaze. I was a most unusual bride but, in this roomful of men, they did not quite know how to explain what was different about me. They cleared their throats and looked obliquely at each other, disturbed by a dim prescience of impropriety.

Then the groom's father, my father-in-law to be, lightly grasped my chin to look into my child-woman eyes, and caught his breath. In the stillness of the hall, I felt a serpentine power sweeping around my heart and squeezing it breathless, silent, just like everyone else.

"I will marry this girl," the groom's father said.

Over the murmurs, I heard my blood rushing into my head and felt the first stirrings of a wild exultation, a sense of power over a man so important. Then Mani pulled me out of the hall and took me down to an empty room, bringing down the heavy wooden bar to latch the door with a heavy thud.

She assessed me for a long time as I kept my head bowed and held my breath, unwilling to betray the excitement bubbling forth, the fear that washed over me in a returning tide.

Mani finally kissed my hair. "There are many kinds of slavery, Shapna. When your husband lets you do whatever you want, it is the greatest freedom of all."

I bent down and touched her feet. Thus was my fate sealed.

Nikhil was forty years old when we married; I was fifteen. I was a child marrying an old man, but no one remembered that when they called me a whore.

Ah, it's getting light outside. There's the pale golden light of a Malayan dawn, do you know it? It's a veiled glow through a misty rain that makes the air translucent with moist edges, as if the gods awaken us with a sprinkle of hallowed waters.

## Twenty-four

Agni lay awake, tossing in sleeplessness. It was too late to get out of the house and see Abhik tonight, but she wanted his arms around her now, telling her that they would be okay. That they were going to be fine.

Abhik was right; she needed to tell her grandmother about their relationship and make it public. Abhik and Agni... Everyone would be *so* delighted. Why was she so terrified?

Why was she thinking about the Professor so often?

*Being old enough to be your father is the big attraction.* She had never had a long term relationship with anyone close to her in age, and Abhik was her first. This was a brand new relationship, not even a year old, started when she hadn't been looking for another man. The four years with Greg had felt like a marriage; the six months with Abhik felt unreal.

The bond with Greg refused to unravel quickly, even though she realised that it was a different Greg she was seeing over the years, not the swaggering American with the fistful of dollars to be thrown at possible danger zones during weekend trips to Cambodia or Myanmar, or any of the tourist destinations in Southeast Asia which had promised more adventure than Holiday Inns. They had gone to those places, where life was cheap and, when fear and weapons met, death was almost a certainty. They had trawled the backyards of shantytowns as enthusiastically as they had the archaeological ruins to taste the essence of a country, not harbouring fear in their heavy backpacks.

Then Greg had gone home, seen the reflection of his mortality in the shattered glass of the Twin Towers more than a thousand miles away, and embraced the certainty of his death. In Malaysia, Greg had faced the inevitability of dying with a sense of procrastination that had allowed him to lead a life unfettered, accepting each new adventure as an affirmation of his being. He who had sauntered into the alleyways of dictators and dervishes, always telling others what could be changed, *must* be improved, was now cowed by the dynastic vengeance in his own backyard. Now his refrain, *Come back with me*, was asking her to die with him a thousand deaths, each colour-coded in a rainbow hue, the red and the yellow and the orange of terror.

She had realised this in the confusion of a night in Ohio ten months ago. Pitch black and cold outside, there had been a lunar eclipse swallowing up the moon in imperceptible bites, gradually. The moon was supposed to turn a livid red but, instead, there had been a gradual darkening until it was gone.

Agni, weary and tired, had stood shivering on the large balcony of the motel. She had asked herself what was waiting at the core of it all, still waiting to be discovered, to make it all bearable. And the darkness and the coldness answered her question: *Nothing*.

Greg had changed, and so had America. She had returned to the room and made love to Greg out of regret and a sense of finality.

Her grandmother's stroke, eight months ago, had brought her back to Malaysia permanently.

Then, one day in April, when the gaiety of the Bengali New Year forced her into another communal gathering in Port Dickson, Agni found herself alone on the beach, fleeing the claustrophobic concern of relatives. The sand was coarse and loose as she walked with difficulty, her feet leaving shallow imprints on the beach. The breeze blew lazy clouds across a sky that was turning dark, swallowing the distant mountains in a blue mist. Far away, she could see some bathers, most likely Malay or Indian women who were fully clothed, and their full skirts billowed like parachutes in the undulating sea.

She had stopped, shocked by the recognition in that scene.

She felt the familiar band around her throat squeezing it tight, leaving her breathless. The women sank with the waves and she closed her eyes.

When she forced them open again, she saw the women rise again and, within the wave that crashed at her feet, she could hear the sound of their laughter – a happy sorority. The pain loosened its grip as she sucked in the salty sea breeze, exhaling the ghost.

New beginnings, she had thought, sinking into the waters of the Straits of Malacca, which washed her clean. Even under the setting sun, sweat beaded her upper lip with a hint of moisture, but the water felt deliciously cool. The waves soaked into her with a sharp rush, and she felt herself sinking into the sand and mudwater.

The wet sand in her cupped palms swirled and clung to her hand. In the breeze she felt the intangible spirit of the land: *I, too, am a child of this soil; I will make it my own.*

*I, too, am a bumiputri.*

It was her history, Indian and Malay and Chinese and much miscegenation, which had been played out on these shores, and she could hear the voice of Shapna, from the depths of a childhood memory:

*In ancient times, ships would set sail from an east Indian port, past the Nicobar Islands, on the breath of the north-east monsoon that breaks in October. From there, they would head for the protected seas west of the island of Sumatra. The Kedah peak stood tall as a landmark from far out at sea, and the sailors used it for navigation. Some ships sailed northwards, to the Isthmus of Kra, where traders would then cross the narrow stretch of land, where they would stay for months, until the winds of the southwest monsoon began guiding them home in May. This was the rhythm of trade, for a mere twelve hundred miles separated ports on the eastern coast of India from the western Malayan ports.*

*In the Bujang Valley, between the Merbok River and Gunung Jerai, there is an archaeological site with ancient temples and Hindu statues and a museum with ancient relics. It's a place where the Indian traders left their footprints from a pre-Islamic age.*

Agni had always made fun of Abhik's involvement in grass-roots groups, teased him about a lawyer's need to chase ambulances in different forms, but maybe, now, it was time for her to try to belong here as much as he did.

More than anything else, since Shapna's stroke, Agni had been hounded by the unanswered questions about her past. Shapna's silence, she knew, meant another chapter closing forever on her own history. It was time for her to find her own answers, to stop running, and make this country her own.

She had her eyes closed but, when she felt another presence, she knew Abhik had come. The slight turbulence in the water touched her before he did.

"Hello Bondhu," he wiped away a wet curl, "You okay?"

He grabbed a fistful of wet sand, slowly releasing it on her hand, the grains of a caress.

She had meant only to nod, but the swell of the sea and the soft mud under her feet made her tumble towards him. He caught her easily, a thumb grazing a breast, and it seemed only natural that she should blend into him, into arms that seemed to fit just right around her body, to press her mouth into his, and let his tongue in. He tasted of the sea, of salt, and earth, and a slight sweet residue. He was real and solid, and Agni, nudged by the waves and the yielding sand under her toes, let herself go, slowly sinking into something which felt like coming home.

The breeze had carried the laughter of the women in *saris*, swimming lazily to shore, their sodden *pallus* like colourful trains behind them.

# Friday

## Twenty-five

He was already an hour late for the Deepavali Open House at his grandparents' home. Abhik sped up the sloping driveway, taking the curve with his foot on the accelerator and swinging the car violently at the apex. The last thing he expected on the top of the drive was the beaten up Peugeot.

"Slow down!" Agni shrieked next to him.

Abhik hit the brakes with the deftness of long practice. The wheels of the BMW churned the gravel as it veered off the road to the right.

The two men standing by the Peugeot glanced up sharply. "Thanks again for the ride," Jay was saying. "I'll see you tomorrow. Thanks for everything..." He broke off as he saw Agni and Abhik approaching. "Agni! And you must be Abhik! Agni, meet Colonel S. We have been colleagues for many years. Colonel S, this is Agni. You knew her mother – Shanti? Shanti and I, if you remember, were very good childhood friends. And this is Abhik."

Abhik shook Jay's hand. "Professor Ghosh, it's great to finally meet you. Colonel S, what an unexpected honour to have you at my family's Open House. *Please* come in."

Colonel S smiled. "Ah, Happy Deepavali my young friend! Unfortunately, I have another prior engagement, so I must wish you Happy Deepavali at your door."

"Please, I insist that you have at least a small drink with us, Colonel, it's the first time you are visiting our home," Abhik urged.

The Colonel was mumbling something when Agni interrupted, a frown lining her forehead. "I have seen you before," she extended her hand, "at the airport?"

Colonel S brushed her hand lightly before touching his heart. "I don't think so," he said evenly.

"Yes," Agni insisted, "at the airport. On Monday. You were there in the evening."

The Colonel laughed easily. "Perhaps old men my age start looking alike," he said. "White hair, sallow skin, stooped back. But I would have remembered a girl as pretty as you, my dear." He turned to Abhik, "I really have to go, young man; I have to travel far. Thank you again for your invitation."

Wishing everyone a cheery Happy Deepavali, Colonel S got into his car and drove off with a beep of his horn. The three of them stood silently and watched as his car spluttered down the driveway.

"He's lying," Agni said through narrowed eyes. "I saw him at the airport."

Jay couldn't curb his annoyance. "Why the hell would he need to lie?"

Abhik adroitly stepped in between them and manoeuvred Agni through the open doorway. "We should go in now, Professor Ghosh. My grandparents are very eager to meet you. Thank you so much for coming."

"I should be thanking *you* for the invitation! Please call me Jay."

"Your parents were my grandparents' friends – so I really should at least call you *mesho* or *kaku* or some sort of uncle?"

*Belligerent Boyfriend.* Jay felt his age highlighted by the younger man's words. Uncle indeed! He could see the beginnings of a smirk on Agni's face; this young man was clearly marking the boundaries with kinship terms.

He smiled broadly. "Please, I insist you call me Jay."

"Okay, if you insist! I am sorry you won't be meeting my parents today. My father is away on his UN assignment for another ten months in Brazil. My grandparents are very eager to meet you though."

The open house was in full swing. Abhik's grandmother, Mridula, was near the door, surrounded by a number of women, but she bustled towards him at once. Jay guessed that Mridula must be at least in her early seventies now, but she was dressed in the colours of a much younger woman. Her slate-grey *sari* had an enormous red border and her jet-black hair was streaked with warm red highlights. Right in the middle of her forehead was an artistically twirled grey curl. Jay smiled as he mused whether the curl changed to match all her outfits.

She returned his smile. "Jayanta!" She raised her hands and clasped his firmly, "I am so glad you could come! I asked Abhik to go fetch you," she looked at Abhik dolefully, "but the children nowadays are *always* too busy."

"No problem at all. A friend dropped me off here," he assured her.

"Come, come, you must meet my husband Ranjan. He has been waiting for you to arrive."

He followed her through the throngs of people, who interrupted their passage with greetings for Mridula, and sized up Jay as he folded his hands in a *namaskar*. She finally stopped next to a bald man in a wheelchair, holding court amongst a large group of other men.

Jay had only a vague memory of the man before him but seeing Ranjan after so many years brought his childhood back again. Ranjan was a documentary filmmaker, and cultivated a certain distinctiveness that had always made him stand out. Jay recognised the elegant figure in his ivory *kurta* with the subtlest of *chikan* embroidery. The *churidar* pyjamas, which folded into waves over his crossed ankles, were of a slightly lighter shade. He seemed as understated as his wife was loud, and Jay felt a rush of affection for this man who had aged so badly.

Ranjan was gesticulating wildly while talking. "The problem,

Oy! – Let me finish here. The problem with us Indians is that we don't think like Malaysians. All Malaysians have the same problem, but these Hindsight 2020 buggers, take the Hindsight fellers, ah, why HIND, like Hindu eh? Why not ask for our rights as Malaysians? We build all these temples here that look like they're from Madras and Rajasthan, for what? We need Malaysian buildings, hah, like the mosque-church-temple *rojak*, and be Malaysian here. You say you want Hindu rights; of course the Muslims don't like it."

"Eh, you think this country is a Petronas advertisement, ah, all *muhibbah* and harmony?" the man on the right interrupted. "That's for TV only, *dey*, all your artsy-fartsy talk cock only. The problem is not about *us* becoming Malaysians. It's whether they see us as foreigners. You think they'll be happy if we build a temple like a mosque, hah? They'll pull it down, say it's an insult. Non-Muslims are not allowed to use the word Allah anymore, *kan*? Go to any country in the West – Europe, America, Canada, or just go down the road only, look at Shah Alam, and you will see huge mosques, round domes, copied from Istanbul or Cairo, all from a glorious Islamic past in another country. Where is the Malaysian in this, hah? Bullshit only!"

"It *was* more *muhibbah* and racial harmony," another man insisted, "in our days, but not any more. We," he stabbed his own chest with a finger twice, "we failed in this... to ask for more... to give our children more."

The man in *batik* stood up. "What, *lah*, you fellers, Malays have been protected under privileges for forty years. *For-ty years*," he emphasised, visibly annoyed. "They don't know the meaning of competition any more. Stop blaming anyone else for their problems!"

Mridula stepped deftly into the middle of the circle and held up her hands. "Quiet!" she hollered. "You all will fight all night about this, so let me introduce you to our *special* special guest, Professor Jayanta Ghosh. We knew him as a small child, running around without any clothes on."

Jay joined in the genial laughter of the men. "It's a pity that you only have this *langto* picture of me in your memory!" he told Mridula reproachfully. Then, turning to the men, he said, "Please call me Jay."

"Welcome back, Jayanta!" Ranjan's clasp was as warm as his voice. "Tell me, how are your parents? And your brother?"

"My parents both passed away," he acknowledged the murmured condolences with a slight dip of his head. "But my brother is well. He is a father of two boys now, and lives in Texas."

"I'm sorry to hear about your parents," Ranjan pointed to his weak legs regretfully, "but really, there's no reason to live at this age, unless you have grandchildren around." He gestured towards Abhik, who was zigzagging through the crowd with two wine glasses in his hand, "That boy keeps me going."

Mridula looked up at Jay. "Don't listen to him. He still has his friends and his beer to keep him happy! But tell me about your own family... Do you have children?"

Jay didn't mention the divorce. Instead, he reached for a picture in his wallet, "We have twin boys, both doctors now. See, here's a picture of Tublu and Gublu at their graduation."

Mridula held up the pictures of the two boys and saw the clear likeness. They looked like Maheshbabu, their grandfather, not so much in their features, but the way they had of looking confidently at the world.

That extraordinary confidence of Maheshbabu. She remembered it well, for it kept them alive during the war.

They looked up to two men in the community then: Nikhil and Maheshbabu. Nikhil was soon stripped of all his authority with the ban on immigration, which left him without a job. Then, with the fall of the British, Nikhil began to drink steadily, reaching for the local *arak* and toddy when all other bottles ran dry.

Maheshbabu kept his sobriety and his dignity through the war years with extraordinary courage. But then, he was not married to Shapna.

Shapna humiliated Nikhil by her affair with Maheshbabu. She behaved like a slut. There was no way to condone that; even though the rot in their marriage, the lack of completion between Nikhil and Shapna, had started with the child that neither could bury, the affair was still unforgivable.

Mridula traced the high intelligent foreheads of the two boys in the picture, remembering Maheshbabu after many years. Shapna had almost destroyed Maheshbabu too.

Mridula sneezed delicately, drawing her *sari pallu* over her shoulder as she watched Ranjan and Jay talking. Jay had been such a tortured teenager. His father and Shapna, carrying on like that, so shamelessly, so openly! She was glad that life had treated him well. Jay's mother, Ila, had borne much, too much for a woman alone in a foreign land to be able to bear.

There was no doubt that Maheshbabu had been a good man. It was Maheshbabu who would appear with offerings from grateful patients, usually Japanese officers, while Nikhil wasted time writing poetry through the war years. Mridula still remembered Nikhil's poem about Chinatown, grim and silent, the deathly hush over Kuala Lumpur, the Chinese eyes through the grilled bars of shophouses.

Mridula looked down at her hands; the memories were so disturbing that she had torn the petals of a marigold to shreds and was now twisting the pliant stem around her finger, like a green ring.

Of course Shapna had been traumatised by the death of her child, she had to give her that. But there had been a world war and a dead child, hah, what was a dead child after all, when the radio wheezed with numbers of the slain? Nikhil was no help. First he blamed himself, then Shapna, for the curse of the malformed child. She remembered the nurse who brought the baby to them saying, *I am not sure how to tell you this. See this banana shape? The baby's head stopped developing at three months, and the spine – it stops here, and then it is all open, only three-fourths formed...*

Then the nurses had all looked at what they called the *specimen,* and she heard the nurse whisper say, *It's all for the best, for everything that happens is destined by Allah.* Nikhil stormed out of the room.

Shapna's best friend, that Malay woman... was it Siti? Yes, Siti, had shouted *Cukuplah!* and hushed them all. She healed Shapna's body with heated stones and tight cloth wraps, plastered her milk with *jamus* that only she knew grew where, stopping the floods, suturing wounds, making her whole. Siti was the only one who dared to come near Shapna as she howled through the nights like a demented amputee, searching for her phantom child, convinced that she had left him somewhere, alone. The others were no one to her; she barely recognised even her husband then.

All war stories are about death and loss. Shapna should not have used that trauma to become so pitiful that a man like Maheshbabu, exemplary in so many ways, left his family for her. It was wrong that Ila, who had agonised about losing Maheshbabu to the war – there were so many ways to die, so sudden and all without warning – had lost Maheshbabu to another woman.

Then there was Maheshbabu's inexplicable decision to take Ila and his two boys to America. No one knew why he had chosen to do that so suddenly. Mridula had once examined Agni's sleeping face and had thought she had seen the reason why, but she held her peace. The truth could be unbearable.

Mridula returned the picture to Jay who looked startled at the interruption. "Your parents," she said softly, "were exceptional people and our *very* good friends." She hugged him tight. "If there is anything we can do for you while you are here, you must, absolutely must, let us know."

# Twenty-six

Watching Mridula's *sari* disappearing into the crowds, Jay realised how tired he was getting of the fractious people around him.

One man was loudly explaining how a minister's Tibetan mistress had been executed by the Malaysian military. Ranjan was simultaneously arguing, on a parallel track, that the Arabs were the most successful colonisers in the history of the world, and had stripped native art forms, rituals, and dressing styles in Malaysia, demanding a loyalty that left no room for the rich layers of the original life. Another man pointed out that all new recruits in any religion, hollowed from the core of their history, found an identity in proving their zeal for their god.

He didn't follow their logic. The country did not appear to be in such a state of heightened lawlessness to him. On the streets, he had seen the covered Muslim women with colourful head-scarves that matched their clothes, not the dark and dour faces of the ninja women that these men were complaining about.

He decided he needed a break from paranoid geriatrics.

He found Agni with Abhik in the wet kitchen. This space, tucked into the back of the house behind the western-style kitchen, was not air-conditioned; it was stifling in the accumulated heat of hot *vadas* being fried. Abhik towered over the catering staff, milling around in their maroon and white uniforms, while Agni unravelled rubber bands from plastic bags holding a variety of sloppy looking sauces. Traces of oily spices pockmarked the marble-topped table, and bits of newspaper were crumpled in random disarray.

"I give up," Agni said. As she raised her hand to wipe off a sheen of sweat, she left a trail of glittering oil. "Shit. Shit!" she shouted, staring at her hands.

Abhik reached over her head for the kitchen towel. Tilting

her forehead with his clean hand, he gently wiped away the smear. "Good as new," he pronounced, "now get back to work, woman; no more excuses."

She stuck her tongue out at him but quickly composed herself as Mridula appeared. "Mriduladida!" howled Agni, "I think I liked it better when you did all the cooking." She switched to a loud Bengali whisper, "These Curries Corner people are absolutely stupid. They need so much help, and work so slowly; then the packets either collapse when you open them, or they burst. This is a stupid, stupid, waste of my time."

"Cheer up, B. We are lucky to have them today, you know that!" said Abhik. He and Agni both noticed Jay at the doorway at the same time.

"Agni," said Jay, "looks like you could do with some help?"

Agni's face brightened, but Mridula was already bustling towards her guest. "Now, Jayanta, you have come after many years; don't waste your time in here. Let me introduce you to someone who knew your parents, a very dear friend of mine. She has been waiting to meet you."

Jay half-turned to see Agni, who, not expecting this act of intimacy to be noticed, ran a deliberate finger down Abhik's groin, leaving a trail of oil. Abhik threw the towel at her and looked down at himself, horrified.

Jay frowned. The situation looked complicated.


"You are working in Nilai tomorrow!" Mridula was saying, "But you can't! You have to come to Port Dickson with us. It has been so many years!"

Jay shrugged, "I want to go, but it's work. Maybe some other time."

"It's an annual event," said the woman who had known his mother. "You *have* to come."

"Stop harassing the man," Ranjan barked from the corner of

the room. "He has important work to do, unlike the rest of us. And the rest of us, well... we are all very hungry!"

Mridula bustled out, but not before glaring at her husband. Jay wandered through the large rooms, catching snippets of conversation, mostly about the politics related to the recent street protests. He stopped at the staircase lined with old photographs, and climbed up two steps to peer closely at the familiar patrician figure.

The sepia-tint had been manually enhanced so that the face had an unnatural pink glow, while the suit had been coloured a bright navy blue. In his right hand the man held a wooden cane, decorated with a glint-eyed hawk head.

Yes. This was definitely Nikhil, Shapna's cuckolded husband. He felt that red-hot hatred flare up after many years. He was amazed that the sight of Shapna hadn't brought on the same intensity of emotion that a picture of her husband had.

There was a burst of loud laughter, and he saw a ring of women sitting under the landing under the stairs. A white-haired woman was saying, "*Tchah*, this grandchild of mine, of course I worry about her! In our time we showed our curves, but we were elegant, hah, flaunting not much skin, but the promise of it, eh?"

"Oh, I've seen *your* pictures! In your time, Nenek," a young women countered, "you all squeezed into bras a size too tight, so that everything spilled out from the transparent *kebayas* yah? Stylo-Milo *lah* you all!" She squeezed her grandmother.

"Such a silly child!" The older woman sighed, "And so naughty! I wouldn't put up with it if it were anyone else!" Her face softened as all the women surrounding her laughed.

Jay turned back to the pictures; he also recognised the old photographs of Ranjan's grandfather and grandmother on the wall. The grandfather was distinguished by a large turban and looked very solemn. His wife, Ranjan's grandmother, had been born in Singapore, and wore a *sari* with a *kebaya* top, the *sari* material bunched around her middle.

Ranjan had started his career in films, so there were frames from the movies lining the stairway. Photographs of the dream merchants of that time, including one from the first Malay movie, *Laila Majnum*, were hung in order. Jay had been a boy of five then, and some of his earliest childhood memories were of the doctor's quarters where his parents had lived for six months, separated from the teeming humanity of the labourers' quarters by a thin wall. This was where the magic of the talking movies first entered his life.

He heard Ranjan's wheelchair approaching, and walked down the steps towards the older man. Ranjan pointed at the picture Jay had been looking at. "I was assisting the Indian film director, Rajhans, in Malaya. Do you remember? Anything from that time?"

Jay spoke rapidly as the memories came flooding back; Ranjan had taken Jay for a shoot one day, and the set was within a large bungalow. When the recording session was on, they had to cover the whole house with large gunnysacks to keep the noise out. It was all very entertaining. Suddenly in the middle of an intense dialogue there would be the ding-ding-ding of the ice-cream man, so they would have to stop. As soon as they started again, an aeroplane would fly past and the director would groan loudly, adding to the noise.

There were lots of songs and dances. These later proved to be a big hit when broadcast on radio but, on the day Jay had gone for the shooting, it seemed more trouble than it was worth. All the songs had to be recorded in one take so, in addition to the incidental noises that disrupted the schedule, any slight mistake by the singer or musicians also brought the session to a halt. The music was performed by violinists, guitarists, and keyboardists, as well as a lone *tabla* player, so he sat impatiently through a number of false starts. Now, dredging from the depths of this memory, he recited a Malay *pantun* hesitantly.

Ranjan clapped the younger man on the back and laughed uproariously. "You probably remember our leading lady, the one with the hibiscus blooms in her hair?"

Jay remembered a lot more. Her tight bustier had left her shoulders bare, and her sarong was wound over a lush body. She was very coy with her co-star, who wooed her with the Malay *pantun*. Jay laughed, "I can't remember all the words any more; but I remember that next to her hibiscus blossoms and her bustier, the poor hero looked quite flat!"

"Yes," Ranjan grew pensive. "That was the golden age of our cinema. This film made good money. People flocked to pay their forty cents and see it."

"So, how long has your family been in Malaya? Looks like your family was here way before Malaya became Malaysia?"

Ranjan pointed at a picture of his great grandfather, standing alone in the frame. "My great grandfather was quite a character. He knifed a friend during a heated argument and ended up in Singapore as a convict, sometime around 1860. Indian convict labour laid the foundations of the roads to Singapore, you know. You can still see the building at the junction of Bras Basah Road and Bencoolen Street. It was a jail once. Almost hidden by palm trees, but still there."

He was distracted by the sound of swift feet as Agni came around the corner. "I'm *hungry*, Ranjandadu," she announced. "Shall we eat now?" She turned to Jay, "The food is being served outside, Professor; please join us."

"Okay, little mother, let's go." Ranjan patted Agni's arm as she steered the wheelchair towards the large French windows. Jay noted their easy relationship. They weren't related by blood, but the kinship in their modes of address to each other spoke volumes about the strength of their ties.

## Twenty-seven

The highway to Ampang was relatively empty, and it didn't surprise Colonel S to be back home in thirty minutes. He stood by the hibiscus tree in the courtyard, drinking in the fresh air on this beautiful day as the air sparkled in bright sunshine. He could see the dark clouds already building up on the far horizon though; the rain would wash away this brightness in the afternoon.

So Jay was celebrating a Deepavali Open House right now, in a home filled with happy Malaysians drinking and eating and laughing together... while this country fell apart.

Colonel S believed that he was the only person in this blighted country who cared in any way. That he was the last Malay patriot, refusing to partake in a celebration that honoured multitudes of copulating deities, in every shape and form, male and female, lion and elephant and fish... It was all so *wrong*.

There was no God but One God, and Allah was without form or gender.

This country was led by a motley crew of wastrels and pimps. It was necessary to periodically remind the infidels that there could be only one real religion in this world, and it was strong. That Malay hospitality for the migrant races shouldn't be taken for granted by the Chinese and Indians; it didn't mean they could do as they pleased in this country. If they didn't like the Malay supremacy, *balik Cina, balik kampong, lah*, just send them back to their own ancestral homes.

He pushed the remote control button and the television sounds filled the room, full of bad news as always. An Indian boy killed in police custody. A Chinese young man found dead outside the office of the anti-corruption agency. A Muslim woman to be caned for drinking beer in a bar. Everything was news.

That female newscaster had a head like a young coconut, filled with fluid, as she cheerfully nodded her way through the miserable broadcast.

Now she was smiling at the Hindsight fellow who was going to have a press conference tomorrow, to demand more rights for the Indian population.

Colonel S stepped closer to the screen. So the Hindsight leader was going to be at the press conference tomorrow? That would give the government a chance to tackle this problem head-on.

Or maybe not.

He heard the Hindsight leader growing more strident, "We are tired of being looked at as 'migrants' instead of 'sons of the soil' like the *bumiputras*... Such categories have no meaning in Malaysia any more! Many of us... the non-Malays... have roots on the Malay Peninsula that go back a hundred years. For the Peranakan Chinese, it's several hundred years, *kan*? In fact, the ancestors of many non-Malays got to Malaysia earlier than the ancestors of many Malays... and changing how we teach history in Malaysia won't change that reality. So we are tired, *lah*, tired of being told that we haven't been there long enough to really be Malaysian like the Malays are. Very racist, like apartheid actually. It's like saying that African Americans are incapable of being true Americans. You see?"

Colonel S glared at the screen. They should have kicked out these migrants as soon as Malaysia gained independence from the British, and sent these British coolies home with their colonial masters. What was this man up to? The Malays would never let there be a Barack Obama situation in Malaysia, not in the next elections, NOT EVER. Go, *lah*, go to America if you want your Martin Luther Kings. No one can stop you from migrating, *kan*?

In those hope-filled days right after Malaysian Independence, when Zainal, Mahesh, and Nikhil had talked into the night, Colonel S was a silent bystander. He resented the way the talk was going, but was too young to object. It was because of the hospitality of men like Zainal that Indians in Malaysia were so arrogant.

Nikhil believed that Malaysians greeting independence with the population equally divided between Malays and immigrant races was a good thing. "Exactly a fifty-fifty split! Time to champion the concept of the multi-racial, non-partisan, New Malaysian."

"Perhaps," Zainal cracked a *keropok* with a loud bite, smiling genially. "Perhaps it will happen. But the Chinese and the Indians are intruders, my friend."

Zainal and Nikhil rarely argued, while Mahesh and Zainal always did, so Colonel S was not surprised to hear Maheshbabu's retort, "*Intruders?* The Indians and Chinese developed this country into what it is. Otherwise the jungle would have claimed you all a long time ago."

"Jungle or not, it belongs to us. Whether we develop, or not, it is our choice," said Zainal.

"Belongs to us, Encik Zainal? You must mean the *Sakais*? By your logic, the aborigines of the country have the greatest claim," Mahesh paused. "But the *Jakuns* – they are not worthy, are they?"

"I do not call them *Jakuns*. You just did." Zainal stopped eating and looked at Mahesh, belligerence in the set of his mouth.

Nikhil smiled at Zainal. "Maheshbhai gets a little hotheaded. You must excuse him. Anyway, we came to Malaya at the invitation of the Malays, and immigrant labour was introduced with their consent, so perhaps intruder is a harsh word, my friend?"

Zainal's eyes remained steadily on Mahesh. He did not

acknowledge what Nikhil had said. Colonel S had swatted a mosquito in the darkness, and felt the satisfying squish of the dead bug under his fingers.

Finally Mahesh had fled to America with his family, soon after that fateful night Zainal and Siti disappeared. What had happened to Zainal was unspeakable, and unforgivable... He could never forget Siti sobbing into his arms *aku dianiaya kawan yang aku anggap darah daging sendiri*... She had treated these people as her own flesh and blood, but been badly betrayed.

Colonel S never allowed anyone from another race to come *so* close. He now increased the volume so that he could clearly hear what the Hindsight leader had to say. The man looked just like a talking baboon on the screen, and should be taken just as seriously.

## Twenty-eight

The sky had darkened with rainclouds. Jay ran his finger lightly around the stem of the chilled beer glass as he admired the setting. Mridula was fussing around the food; her flamboyant *sari* heaved around her curves with every breath.

The air was slightly moist with the hint of fog. Even though it was only late afternoon, fairy lights twinkled at strategic places in the garden, the highlight of which was an enormous man-made waterfall, backlit to maximise the majesty of the gushing water. Besides the sound of the water, there was the zap of insects being lured into the neon traps and the low nasal humming of the mosquitoes. The table was loaded with an excess of dishes that slowly congealed in the cool air.

"It must be impossible to get bad food in Malaysia," Jay remarked.

Ranjan cocked his head and addressed the statement in all seriousness. "Except at one time. During the war years there was no food, and whatever we did get was exceptionally bad."

Mridula nodded her head. "Jayanta, the food was so scarce that our code words were the common foods that no one ate any more. We ate only tapioca, sweet potatoes and yams. If we spoke of putting *brinjals* in a *shukto*, there was no guessing; everyone knew it wasn't the food being discussed."

"So exciting, *lah*! All this hide-and-seek," Agni said with a shiver.

Mridula exchanged a glance with Ranjan and snorted, "You all, hah! You find it so romantic-shomantic, all talk only with eyes shining like two black pearls. But we, who took risks with our lives and saw death day in and day out, found it hateful – anything but exciting! Babies dying –" Mridula broke off sharply.

Ranjan cleared his throat. "We should talk about things which are more pleasant, eh?"

Agni stopped eating as Abhik advanced, a heavy plate of mutton *periyatel* balanced on his palm, enroute to Jay. He had changed into dark slacks from the jeans he had worn in the kitchen. He placed the plate carefully in front of Jay, and turned to his grandparents, kneeling on the grass so that his face was level with his grandfather.

"I have some bad news. I can't come with you to Port Dickson tomorrow. I'm really sorry. The Hindsight 2020 leader is flying back from London, and the press conference is tomorrow morning. I have to be there, in case the police try anything." He looked at Agni, then at his grandparents. "I'm *very* sorry, I just found out about this. I'll try to get to PD as soon as I can."

Ranjan's face was stony. In profile, anger chiselled his features until they seemed to pierce the air. "Even Agni took leave from such an important press conference at the airport tomorrow. Surely you can do something? No! It's wrong that they cannot leave you alone even for our religious celebrations. And you, out there with all the ruffians who claim to protect us."

"There's nothing you can do?" Mridula asked.

One of Ranjan's friends put a hand on the old man's arm. "Let it be. You all should be proud that he is trying to make a difference. He is getting involved with the Hindsight fellers to fight for us. We never got involved, but maybe we should have, my friend."

Ranjan spun the wheelchair around to face his friend. "Of course I am proud of Abhik. I cannot live without him, but his work is too much! These people have no respect —" Ranjan took a deep breath and squeezed his grandson's fingers. "Just come to Port Dickson as quickly as you can, okay?"

Mridula's hands rested on her husband's shoulders, gently. Her veins stood out under gnarled joints, and her fingers were emphasised by an unusually large number of rings. Almost every finger except the thumb had a ring.

The two Malay girls who joined the group broke the sombre spell.

"Hello Rohani and Shiraz! Good to see you both after such a long time!" Mridula embraced them both with expansive arms.

The girls smiled at Ranjan, hugging Mridula. Then with a "Happy Deepavali, everyone!" they settled into the space created for them.

At some point in the early evening, a group of women had gathered at the open foyer to begin preparations for the lamp-lighting. Agni was now dressed in a turquoise *sari* with an intricate gold border that glittered, and Jay marvelled at the transformation. She dazzled without the least trace of self-consciousness. Jay searched for the denim-clad coquette that he identified with.

She and two other Indian girls knelt on the floor, lighting the hundred and eight lamps that had been placed in the pattern of an *Om*. Pink and green lotus buds, in huge clusters, peeked from over her shoulder as she tiptoed around the intricate *alpona* design, which already showed signs of smearing. The *diyas* flickered prettily, casting shadows on her features. Jay caught his breath at the beauty of the spectacle.

He eased himself into a low rattan armchair, which was comfortably antique. This was the first time in his life he had met such a chameleon woman, one who would be at ease in all his worlds. A Malaysian woman like Shanti, but one who would not drown, leaving him with demon teeth for a memory. Someone who had also been abandoned, was flawed, and was still looking for the sum of her parts... like him.

"Enjoying yourself?" Abhik had a hand on the rattan chair as they watched the same woman.

"It's all very... magical. Somehow I didn't expect so much feeling. In North America they have huge *pujas*, often held in gyms and church halls, and I've been squirted with *ganga jal* from a squeezee bottle," he laughed. "This neighbourhood community thing feels very different."

"I don't know for how much longer though," said Abhik reflectively. He indicated the older women who had clustered around the central area, telling the younger women what to do. "Those are our gatekeepers and keep this going. After them, the next generation is all working women, with little time for rituals."

Agni looked across at them both enquiringly. Abhik raised his thumb to his lips to ask whether she wanted a drink.

She made her way across the room, and flopped into a chair. "Could you get me a rum and coke? Easy on the rum, or I'll trip on the yards of fabric, and your grandmother won't be amused. This is some family heirloom I am wearing."

Abhik grinned. "What can I say? She's keeping things in the family."

The implication was unmistakable, but Jay refused to ask any questions even as Abhik walked away. He turned to Agni. "Look, I'm sorry about getting a little snappy about Colonel S. Old men of his age do start looking alike. Trust me, he hasn't left the house for months. He had problems starting his car when I first met him at his house. The battery was almost dead."

"He lied," Agni said dismissively. "I saw him at the airport on Sunday. He is on our surveillance cameras."

"Why would he need to lie to you?" Jay asked reasonably.

"I don't know. Rohani is standing in for me for the rest of the week, so I can go to Port Dickson tomorrow. But, as soon as I come back, I'll find out." She stood up abruptly.

"Well, in that case, good luck. I am pretty sure you'll find someone else on your footage."

"How are you so sure? How well do you know this guy anyway?"

Jay let the silence grow as he controlled his anger. "I've known him all my life. He saved me from the fire – yes, the one you asked me about earlier – then he set me up in a lab in Seattle and taught me everything I know about science. Whatever I am today is thanks to him. He has been mentor, friend... father." His voice dropped, "I know him very well.

The call to the faithful rang out over the noise of the guests. Stereophonic sounds of *Allah hu akhbar* rose and fell like the wingbeats of the birds in the darkening air as they stared at each other.

Finally, Agni looked away. "In that case, Professor, I really hope I am wrong."


Jay watched Abhik and Agni from a distance. In her gregariousness, and his quietude, he saw an edge of insecurity that separated them. It was obvious that their relationship hadn't been made public. He could hope.

A young man was intoning like a Bollywood hero, "Hai, if you ever get tired of waiting for your prince, I am always here. I even wrote a sonnet to read out this evening."

"*Aiyah*, not another *Desire on Deepavali*," Rohani mimed finger-in-throat gagging.

Agni's laughter pealed out as she reached for the glass Abhik handed her. "Don't waste it on me! My mother was the poet; my networks involve computers, not people. No time for love, *lah!*"

The next door neighbour, Mrs Wong, had seated herself next to Agni and was sharing a bowl of *murruku* with her. Jay heard Agni's giggles over Mrs Wong's voice. "Love shove, pah! That's the trouble with all you youngsters! You think Mr Wong and I got love when we married? Never even see each other properly before the wedding day, now married for forty years already. No need for love-one, you take it from me. Find a good boy, family good, can earn some money, enough what?"

And Mrs Wong looked meaningfully at Abhik.

Agni nudged Abhik with her shoulder. "*Chee*, what are you saying? Marry my brother? Cannot, *lah*!"

Mridula, who was re-filling the bowl of cashew nuts, frowned. She wagged her finger, "There is no blood shared between you and him. You take a lamp and search the whole world, girl; you'll never find another diamond like this one. There is no problem of suitable girls for *him*!"

"Mriduladida! If you matchmake us all the time, I'll go away!" Agni stood up and pouted, her hair in little curls over her face. Turning slightly cross-eyed, she blew one away from the tip of her nose as she shook her head, a charming vision of wild womanchild. Abhik hid his face in his hands and groaned, but Agni didn't seem at all disconcerted. She poked Abhik in the ribs. "Get married quick, Casanova," she said, "or the relatives will be scooping up corpses of girls flinging themselves at you."

She flung an arm on the coffee table to highlight her comment, and dislodged the *murruku* bowl, strewing the contents on the floor. "Oops!"

Two maids were at the spot almost immediately, clearing up the mess. Jay stepped over the mess to approach the group. "I have to leave now. Thank you so much for your hospitality."

"You must stay a bit longer!" Mridula insisted. "Especially as we won't be seeing you at Port Dickson tomorrow! We hardly had a chance to talk properly. I've been so busy supervising in the kitchen..."

"I wish I could, but I have an early appointment." He clasped Ranjan's and Mridula's hands warmly in goodbye. "I'll be back soon! This feels like home already."

# Twenty-nine

Agni and Abhik watched Jay leave the room. "Why are relationships so complicated?" Agni asked softly.

Abhik felt his heart pounding but he just raised his eyebrows.

"My grandmother and his father being together... while his mother was around... Can you imagine what he went through as a kid? He must have been so traumatized – but, strangely, it was my grandmother who was agitated at seeing *him*."

"Was she?" He tried to keep his voice level. "So long ago already, and," Abhik paused briefly, "it's none of our business. Consenting adults and all that. If the talk in Pujobari didn't bother them, and they carried on anyway, you shouldn't let it get to you now." He looked at her closely and sighed. "Hah! I knew it! You don't owe him anything, B. Not an apology, and especially not your guilt."

Agni took a deep breath. "All my life I have had to deal with such traitorous thoughts about Dida, and now that he's come back, that's the only thing on my mind."

"Traitorous?"

"About me, mainly. About Dida making people around her do exactly what she wanted, like not letting my mother marry my Malay father. While she went ahead and carried on with a married man... Maybe my grandmother didn't do me a favour by bringing me up. If I had a Malay father, I would be entitled to more from this country. Maybe I would have the arrogance to march out of a meeting whenever I wanted."

"March out of a meeting? Is that the sum of your ambition, Bondhu?"

"Of course it's more than that!" Agni snapped. "And now the Professor's here," she said, "I see someone like me. You know, broken... He seems broken somehow."

"And you think you can fix this broken old man?"

Agni looked away. "I'm the last person who can fix anyone. I should just fix me first, find out who I am. It's time I looked for my father."

Abhik thought for a while. "Isn't he somewhere in Kelantan?"

"I don't know. I should find out. I thought I could run away from all this while I was with Greg, you know? New country, new people, but the problem is *inside* me."

"Not a problem, Agni. Just missing pieces."

"Right. Anyway, I want to stop trying to blank out my history. I love this country and, as I get older, I think this is the only place in the world that will ever feel like home."

"Home? Imperfect, unfair..." Abhik recited, counting off the fingers of his hand.

Agni grinned in agreement. "Yep! Imperfect, unfair... but my very own."

"Okay, Bondhu," said Abhik. "Then join one of the groups that are making a difference. I am serious! Otherwise you'll be singing *Rasa Sayang* during the open house season and griping the rest of the year again."

"At least I'm back here. It's better than just quitting and leaving, like so many of us are doing?" Agni looked at Abhik archly.

"*Touché,*" said Rohani from behind. "Hey, you two, want to get a drink at Bukit Hartamas and then head home? A Deepavali treat from me?"

"I can't," said Abhik, "It's my party; can't leave if I want to."

"I'd love to go," Agni squeezed Abhik's arm. "I've been behaving the whole day, and it'll be nice to chill with Rohani for a while. Pick me up on your way back to the apartment?"

Mridula emerged from the doorway to wag a finger in Agni's face. "Leaving already? It's high time you got married, and started hosting some of these parties, so old women like me can get a break!"

Agni hugged Mridula tight. "You old, Mriduladida? You'll outlive us all. Byeeee!"

"*Chee*, grumbled Mridula, kissing Agni on the cheek, "what inauspicious things you say, *shaitan*!"

Another quick squeeze and Agni was gone, leaving the fragrance of jasmines. Mridula turned to Abhik, "That's what Shapna and Siti were like. One Malay, the other Indian, yet the best of friends. *Durga*, *Durga*, I hope this friendship lasts for ever."

Abhik put an arm around his grandmother's shoulders. "No reason not to! They're very different though, with Rohani so gentle from growing up in a Malay household with all that *adat*. It's a beautiful thing."

Their conversation was interrupted by flashing lights and a toot-toot of the horn as Agni and Rohani drove off.

# Thirty

Jay sat in the cavernous office at Nilai, the dark corners of the former factory sheathed in blackness. His lone table was illuminated by a table lamp that cast a round spot of illumination on the sheaf of printouts.

Jay peered at his screen in disbelief. Was this an elaborate hoax of some sort, or something more real on a scale that could plague the rest of his academic career?

Neurotic *Neka*, he scolded himself. Get a grip.

His self-diagnosis had shadowed his childhood. He had always been a total pessimist, the *Lone Loser*. All through college, life was a contest for things that eluded his grasp; but he had learnt that very early, in Malaysia, from Shanti. He excelled academically for an absentee father who would, invariably, remind him of his *Spare* status.

His brother, *The Heir,* called him *neka*, a Bengali term that labelled him both effeminate and pretentious, in one precise bisyllabic word. His brother was happily married, and had heirs of his own now, even as Jay still trawled through the world like a teeming raincloud, waiting for release. His brother, throughout his whole life, had seemed undiminishable by anything. But then, his brother had never been abandoned in a fire, left to the kindness of strangers. His brother had been picked up in their father's arms and carried to safety, out of the amusement park, that fateful day. He closed his eyes and felt his finger tracing agitated circles in the air.

Unlike his brother, Jay had grappled with women who gave too much too soon and then gave up too soon. The Indian women in America had intimidated him in his early twenties, for they were nothing like the women he had known in the small towns of Malaysia. No matter how many traces he found, no one came close to Shanti. His mother would host lavish dinners, where, delicately dabbing a corner of her lips with a precisely folded handkerchief, she would say, "Well, my husband, he is such a busy doctor, you know..." and vaguely wave her hands in the air. That was all she needed to validate herself and her family, even when they were living in the ghettos of New Jersey, while his father retook multiple exams to prove his medical knowledge.

Then the Bengali women started wearing chunky black oxidised metal jewellery, and stylishly enormous dots on the centre of their foreheads, and said dismissively, "I'll get this doctorate from Columbia even if it kills me," and his mother had nothing left to say. These creatures in sleeveless blouses and see-through chiffons that bared their belly buttons agitated his safe world, even as his mother, in her heavy *Tanchoi* silks, was diminished.

When his mother found Rina for him, he was already in his late thirties. Rina was visiting her older sister for the summer in Seattle, and they both pretended it was love at first sight instead of an arranged marriage.

They were separated now, he and Rina. Their twin boys, too, had their own careers now. He had lived apart from their mother for so long that he had never really figured in their lives. He regretted that now, but his own non-relationship with his father had given him the template for dealing with his sons.

By the time the boys were toddlers, Rina had accepted the inevitability of Jay's detachment. They had seen too many couples entering into commuter marriages to keep pace with changing job markets, or stuck in flagging relationships, all ending in divorce. Then their careers had taken off as Jay was recognised globally as one of the foremost experts in biomaterials, and Rina had done well as a realtor over the years. They had begun to relish the freedom from couplehood that was possible in America. As long as they limited their contact with the Indian community, there were no prying questions. They had tried to keep their marriage outwardly intact, at least for the children, as divorce seemed like an unnecessary complication. When the twins were still living at home, Jay was a guest speaker at their schools frequently so that the boys could be publicly fathered in his fame.

Rina didn't bother about his women. She understood that first Jay loved only Jay, then his work, then the boys, then his mother, then Rina. A new woman usually placed seventh on his list. When Manjula Sharma had come into Jay's life, Rina expressed a deep pity for this woman whose eyes had sparkled so brightly at the camera.

But now – finally! – Jay had found someone else like him, in fact even more flawed. Maybe he could finally stop flagellating himself.

He forced himself to look at the screen in front of him again. The collage of pictures: a Tibetan model, black hair gleaming against white orchids in her hair, standing by the Potala Palace with the sun shining blindingly off her intricately-worked silver belt; a fuzzy picture, in Paris, the model with a politician; a barren field with burnt dark patches; a piece of dark cloth, lying on the ground like furry batwings. And below it all, the blogger had posted a document that said in a clear black-and-white type:

*My informer states that Colonel S was the person who placed the C4 on various parts of the victim's body...*

Jay clicked on the various tabs, all blogs related to Colonel S, and the murder of a Tibetan model. Page after page of the role of Colonel S in the greater political scheme of things. Some of the attacks were vicious opinions; others were substantiated with documents and photographs.

Of all people, it was Manju who had alerted him to this. Manju, whom he had left behind in Boston, sure that they were over, no chance of a reconciliation no matter how much she begged, had written him an email. It was a Manju Mail, full of snide allusions to the ghosts he was still battling, to his impotency in all things... and he had almost deleted that vomit. Then, towards the end, Manju the Poet had written a crude doggerel, saying:

> You think your colonel's such a hero,
> Buddy, watch your ass, he's more like Nero,
> Fiddling while a country burns...

He had decided to Google the Colonel with the aim of writing an equally bad-versed reply, telling her how wrong she was. Instead he had stumbled upon this cyberspace of incriminatory evidence.

Jay felt ill. He would never have thought to Google Colonel S by himself; he had known the man practically all his life! No one Googled an avuncular figure who had been a mentor to boot, someone who had rescued Jay from a life dependent on happy drugs to get through the day and given him a career he actually wanted to wake up for.

He thought one knew all there was to know about such a saviour. Clearly not. *Masked Mentor*.

In his ears, he heard the conversation at the Open House, the allegations about a military style execution of the model. He remembered Agni's face, turning away from him and saying, *In that case, Professor, I really hope I am wrong*.

Jay paced around that solitary puddle of light from his table. What was he supposed to do now? Confront the guy? If this was true, Colonel S would never admit it but, if were untrue, would so many bloggers write about it?

He stumbled on a brick on the floor and found himself flailing in the dark. He felt physically and mentally confused, with no one he could turn to for advice. It seemed significant that the only one who had warned him about such a danger to his career was someone who did not wish him well. He had not felt so alone, or more friendless, all his life.

An hour later, looking through all the research specifications on the printouts, his sense of unease about this project coagulated into anger. He should have known better.

Jay's expertise was in designing and modifying polymers for biomedical applications. Hemocompatibilisation of polymers had been showing promising breakthroughs, but the only thing that Colonel S seemed to be interested in was the fully biodegradable stent technology. The specifications for what was required for the Malaysian study did not indicate any medical use. It was clearly not going to be used either for gene or drug delivery.

So what else *was* there? What was Colonel S up to?

Yesterday, he had spent much time on a demonstration of the crimping and expansion test. He thought of the burnt field, the eyes of the dead Tibetan model, the black cloth on the ground. How was this related to his own research?

He had left the lab in Seattle when he realised that his mentor's research in Materials Science was straying into obscure military applications. Once it became clear that Colonel S was growing disinterested in medical applications, Jay had found a reason to leave. At that time, there had been vague hints about developing a cache of superexplosives to be carried within the human body, but Jay had left before the questions became too difficult.

*Hutang emas boleh di bayar, hutang budi di bawa mati. Debts of gold can easily be repaid; debts of gratitude are carried to the grave.* He had been taught this Malay saying too early in his life to ever forget it. He could not turn against Colonel S.

Jay felt the agitated circles of his finger as an image of Agni, lit up in the glow of one hundred and eight lamps, crossed his mind. He had left the party about three hours ago, but it felt another world away.

He couldn't leave Malaysia again, not just now.

Which meant he would have to find out what Colonel S was really doing. His mind whirled with possibilities: the street protests in Kuala Lumpur; the elections in a few months; deaths at the anti-corruption agency. Where was the next military application?

If Colonel S was insisting on his working quickly, it wouldn't be long in coming.

This country was such a cesspool. He had forgotten all that suspicion of other races beneath the polite veneer, how quickly something became a problem and had to be countered.

His father, influenced by Shapna, had been the worst when it came to suspecting the motives of the Malay race. He had seen it all clearly during a trip to Bali.

Looking back at that trip, the adult Jay now realised that his father had been trying out his mistress as wife material.

Jay's mother, Ila, had left for India. Jay couldn't remember when or why she had done that – he had been too young – but he had woken up one morning to find her gone. Then his father had taken the two boys and Shapna to Bali.

Bali brought Shapna's history books alive and transformed her. She delighted in the simplicity of Bali, even in the pesky barefoot children who wouldn't leave them alone. They took a tourist coach and saw the volcanoes, and the terraced *padi* fields and, finally, they stopped at the 14th century Tanah Lot temple.

The Hindu shrine shimmered at the edge of the beach, high on a hill like a particularly glorious gem growing more beautiful with age in its perfect setting. Shapna sat on the beach, leaning on the tiny cave that the touts claimed was filled with serpents, and cried with sheer joy. When Jay poked a furtive hand into the cavern, he found nothing.

Shapna turned to Mahesh and said, "*This* is what I wanted to see in Malaya: the Shiva and Vishnu shrines that once stood on Kedah Peak; statues from the Gupta period in Perak." She shut her eyes, and wriggled her toes into the wet sand of the beach in sheer bliss.

"We learnt about the Sri Vijaya Empire in school," Jay offered his father this nugget of information.

Shapna blew the sand out of a conch shell she had found, and asked instead, "And what did you learn, child?"

Jay puffed up his chest at this chance to impress his father. Then he recited, "The king converted to Islam through a dream. *Recite the words of faith,* he was told in the dream. When the ruler replied that he did not know how, the person asked him to open his mouth and spat into it. *A taste rich and sweet.* When the ruler woke up, he saw that he was circumcised, and could recite the words of the Koran. *Tantaraa!*" He finished with a flourish, proud of his knowledge, but Mahesh's eyes had narrowed into slits that glared, *You stupid halfwit.*

"Spat into his mouth?" Mahesh foamed, "And all this magic makes perfect sense to you? So much magic; is this what you swallow in school?"

Shapna had turned and absentmindedly begun to draw curlicues of her own name in Bengali in the sand. Mahesh raged, "History! Written when the splendor of the Malaccan court had declined, and Malay kings were harried by the Portuguese and Acehnese... when distortion became necessary, even though the claims were absurd."

A strong gust of wind whipped Jay's hair, slapping his forehead with a sudden sting. Rainclouds gathered over the horizon, at the edge of which balanced two little girls, pink and purple spades in hand. They laboured on a sandcastle with a black pebble wall, even as the sea rushed in stealthily, filling the sinuous moat. An empty packet of twisties whirled a jagged orange and green somersault through the breeze as his brother chased after it.

Shapna's voice took over, singsong, rising and falling like the waves spitting white foam bubbles at their feet. "The Gujarati seamen came in heavy *dhows* loaded with tons of cargo, the timbers lashed together, unriveted by metal to avoid the risk of rusting. During the long voyage, the sailors rode these slippery logs with desperately splayed toes. Many fell to their deaths as the structures unravelled in heavy storms. Ah, child, this country was such a marvellous crossroad of cultures, such a mingling of bloods!"

In Shapna's voice, Jay could smell the burnt incense, hear the bustle of the arrival, unloading and reloading of hundreds of ships. He saw the elephants, owned by the fat Gujarati merchants, lumbering between seamen.

But his father brought them back to the moment with the sharpness in his tone. "No magic here, just the cycle of history! I wish we could *feel* this history in Malaysia, but there are no Tanah Lots there, eh?"

Shapna said gently, "Ancient history, *tcha*, it is so easily forgotten!"

"Not forgotten. Erased. If we all pretend it never happened, maybe it didn't," said Mahesh.

Shapna sighed deeply. "Until the river floods and the silt uncovers what should remain hidden."

Jay had looked at her quizzically. He was about to ask her which river was going to flood, but the tour guide hurried them back into the bus.

It would be too many years before he would find out exactly what Shapna had meant, and by then it would be too late and his life would have changed forever. In this cesspool of a country, too much was covered up by muddy rivers that did not flood.

But Colonel S? He had been a father figure for Jay, when his own father had given him the crumbs of his attention, or whatever was left after Shapna had finished. Depression and mood-enhancing drugs plagued his years in America until Colonel S had found him a place in that lab in Seattle. Then science had given his life such a meaning and validity that his human relationships paled in comparison.

He could never turn against Colonel S, no matter what happened. He always had the option of leaving if things became too uncomfortable again.

First, he would have to ask some oblique questions, digging into the specifications of the research but also reading much more into what was left unsaid. Until then, there was all this work to finish, until late into the quiet night.

# Thirty-one

Agni and Rohani turned into Desa Hartamas, a hip yuppie kingdom where Japanese and Mexican restaurants competed for customers with the nostalgic Malayan *kopitiams* from the Fifties. A parking spot seemed impossible until a *jaga kereta* squeezed them in between a Jaguar and a Proton Perdana.

"Make sure no one scratches my car, okay?" Rohani dropped some coins into his palm. He nodded automatically, shifting his gaze to the cars coming in.

Rohani had enveloped the car in the essence of roses and minty mouthwash. She indicated the *jaga kereta* boy with her head and said cheerfully, "The doped-out dregs of KL, but still useful!"

Agni felt cheered just looking at Rohani. She had on a romantic rebel outfit, a frilly soft muslin shirt with pants studded with zippers, and some serious shoes. Agni envied the way Rohani's skin shone with a milky translucence. "You look so right for this place," she commented wryly. "In my antique *sari*, I look like your auntie, *lah*!"

"Don't be silly, Agni. No one's looking anyway. And be careful with that beautiful fabric; you're trailing it on the ground!"

Rohani was mistaken; they were attracting quite a bit of male attention. Agni glared at the moony drunkard sitting in the corner, and lit a cigarette as soon as they sank into their seats.

Rohani blurted out. "I got the offer letter – MBA, Wharton."

Agni squealed in delight, "Congratulations! Why didn't you tell me earlier?"

"It's been pretty crazy at work, yah?" Rohani shook her head, "And you were so busy with the employee clearances, worrying about Abhik and Hindsight... Didn't seem the right time to share the good news."

"Sorry, *lah*! But this is great news, and you'll be with Sven again! *Aiyah*, but you're doing so well here, major media star and all – I haven't had time to read the piece, but there was some magazine article last week?"

"Oh, that rubbish? Nothing much – one of the Malay women's magazines just did a spread. Crusader Sister or some such headline, about my work with the Sisters in Islam."

"Oooh. I haven't picked up a Malay magazine in ages, but I'll have to see this!"

Rohani stubbed out her cigarette. "Don't bother. They have a butt-ugly picture of me. I think they didn't know whether to do a prodigal daughter story or a black sheep angle."

A waitress appeared. "*Minum*?" she asked, swabbing the table with a stained grey rag.

"*Teh tarik?*" Rohani asked. Agni nodded and, as Rohani placed an order for two drinks, Agni listened to the gentleness in her manner of address. *Kak*, she called the waitress, and her voice lilted in entreaty rather than command. Such small courtesies refined over centuries of civilisation resulting in such gentle dignity; Agni was charmed by the musicality of Rohani's manners. Rohani's family traced its roots to a Malaccan court. When a throne fell vacant, the Bendehara were the kingmakers, often providing consorts for the king from their own eminent family.

"God, I'll miss this place!" Rohani sank lower into her seat.

"You'll come back. You've done it before!"

"I don't know, Agni." Rohani drew a long breath. "My brother, you know, the politician, the one I'm staying with now? His wife bothers me all day with *haram* this and *haram* that. I'm finding it hard to be myself in my own family now."

"Excuse me?" Agni raised a disbelieving eyebrow, and took a sip of the hot tea.

"You have no idea, obviously; you can do as you want. One Muslim woman might get caned for drinking in public, yah, so what does that do for those of us who like pubs? I've had it up to here trying to figure out what *might* offend someone next... too much tension."

Agni sighed. "I try to keep out of all this and just concentrate on work, but Abhik makes me feel really selfish."

Rohani laughed. "Oh, I just love Abhik!" She leaned forward conspiratorially, "How're things with you two, eh? You may not be telling me, girlfriend, but something's going on there, yah?"

Agni smiled mysteriously. Rohani grabbed her arm and made a face, "So tell, *lah!*"

Agni began the story with the kiss in the waters of Port Dickson. The rain poured noisily down while the streetlamps, murky yellow spills in the blackness, lit up the spray like ghostly sprites dancing in the air. They watched the wind picking up the dust like a carpet, flinging it onto windshields and the trees.

"So that's all, nothing much to tell."

"Yah, nothing much to tell!! Congratulations!"

"Actually, it's all too new. I don't want to talk too much, okay? Not yet."

"Okay. Got it."

There was a contemplative silence. "So how about you? What's next with Sven?" Agni asked her.

"Let's see. I'm going back to the States, even if it feels all fucked up there sometimes. It's saner than here, you know. Easier to have desires."

"Unless you're gay in certain states," said Agni. "But they did just legalize gay marriage."

Rohani smiled naughtily. "No king-sized mattresses being hauled into courts there!"

Agni reacted to her flippancy. "The Anwar case wasn't about sex! It was politics that only you Malays could talk about. The rest of us just sat in front of our TV screens and watched with our mouths shut."

The silence grew as the smoke from Agni's cigarette whispered past the neon sign flashing LAW HAIRDRESSING, and hung suspended for an instant around the gaudy green light. Then the thunder and lightning pierced the world. A shrub writhed in the wind, its leaves tickled and convulsed in delight – until the darkness shrouded it again.

"Actually, I reacted to the sex more than the politics in the Anwar case."

"What?" Agni stared at her.

"Well, homosexuality makes me uncomfortable." Rohani shrugged self-consciously. "I don't know why, it just does." She held up a hand to stall the interruption. "I just don't believe it's okay for all consensual adults to have sex. Let's draw out the parallel. Is it okay for adults to have incestuous sex? Like brother and sister, mother and son? Let's say possible pregnancies are taken out of the equation. So if any two adults have consensual sex, is it okay?"

"Incest is never okay. You can't compare like that!"

"Well, incest was okay for the pharaohs... and the Mughals too. For me, gay sex is eeeeww. So it's all quite relative, pun intended."

The TV, droning on in a corner of the coffee shop, caught their attention with a news flash. "Anyway, at least the political players are changing now. Probably the filthiness in Malaysian politics will get better." Agni said.

Rohani grimaced. "It will get a lot worse before it gets any better," she said grimly, "*especially* with the Indian agitation."

She wiped her grimy fingers on the edge of a napkin, carefully folding the greasy part out of sight. "My parents were open-minded, very liberal, yah? Wanted us to mix with all races, study abroad and all that; be globally Malay. But you know why I went to an international school?"

"Same as me, I guess," said Agni, "to get an English education?"

"No, *lah*! Nothing that simple. I was considered un-Islamic in my other school, for things like wearing shorts during hockey practice, and not wearing a headscarf, everyday things."

Agni started to laugh.

"It wasn't funny to my parents. My mother went to complain, you know, about the ridiculousness of it all, but when she parked her car, the *ustazah* heard *Hotel California* on the car radio. She was so angry; such music is *haram* we were told, like taking drugs."

Agni looked at Rohani steadily. "That was *one* crazy teacher you had."

"Agni, you have no idea. And it was just the beginning. My niece was told off for using chopsticks, so un-Islamic, how can – ! My parents think it's just getting worse."

Agni ground her cigarette and waited for Rohani to continue.

"So," said Rohani quietly, "everyone thinks Malays are too stupid to be dangerous. And we get quietly hijacked by the radicals."

"Too heavy, *lah*, this conversation," said Agni.

"Anyway, I feel I can do more if I stay in the US, you know; help change the direction things are moving in globally right now."

Agni sat up. "What about making a change here? Making things better here?"

"Change?" Rohani snorted. "I'll leave it to my politician brother. It's his job."

Agni didn't even smile at her sarcasm.

"Ahh, Agni. I am just waiting for the wheel to turn full circle. I can't handle all this stuff with *haram* this and *haram* that. That's why I joined the Sisters in Islam – to make sense of some of it. I can't even argue with my family because that proves how the West has corrupted me. But I grew up with stories of magic and sex as facts of life. Nowadays, we are told that if we dress this way and pray five times, that's the only magic to wipe out all evil. I'm running off overseas again."

"You've really agonised about this."

'Well I *care* about what is happening! My mother's family followed the matriarchal system from Sumatra, and property passed from mother to daughter. Now, as soon as my cousins get married, they change into docile wives. This change is not what I want, but what to do?" She looked over Agni's head and leapt to her feet. "Hey, loverboy's here!"

She rushed past Agni. Agni swivelled in her chair to see Abhik envelop Rohani in a deep hug. Then Rohani said something into his ear that made him grin at Agni.

## Thirty-two

*It is almost midnight and Agni is not home. I worry about her, at that party all day with Jay, and what he is whispering into her ears. He will not leave until he has destroyed her.*

*I worry about her. The streets are uneasy again. The Tamil nurse has dragged the small TV into this room and watches the screen all day; she is slopping the medicines into my mouth without checking the labels. Just an hour earlier she was giving me water to swallow my pills and was so mesmerised by the TV that the water dribbled into a pool at my neck, soaking the collar of one of the new maxis which Agni bought last week.*

*The new maxis are very pretty, all three of them, in pastel shades of pistachio, pink, and lavender, my favourite colours. As my pink maxi was getting ruined, I was so upset I gagged because I couldn't shout, but the nurse was irritated at the mess as if it was my fault. She twisted the collar as though to wring my neck. I am resigned to this. When you are old, you pay for curses and shifting moods, living on the scraps of kindness from those you employ.*

*The streets are uneasy again, just as they were when Jay left the last time. He has returned to finish the job he left unfinished because his parents fled so soon after the riots of 1969. But I will not think of him as a fire-breathing deathgiver; oh no, nothing so powerful when he is only the scum of the earth.*

*Maheshbabu had to leave this country because of Jay. He left me because of his son's vengeance. I have no illusions about this, although people like Mridula and the other Bengali women will tell you Maheshbabu left because he repented. They will tell you that Ila returned from India because she loved her sons too much to stay away, and that she came back to her husband who welcomed her with open arms.*

*All lies.*

*Ila had given up Maheshbabu almost as if she was delighted to* release him. In one stroke she had cut through the knot of their marriage and set him free so that she would never again share his bed, a meal, or anything remotely marital. He didn't matter any longer, so his relationship with me was of no consequence.

And Maheshbabu? He twined me closer to him in response, especially after Nikhil passed away. As much as I had hated Nikhil's distance, his hiding in his poetry and his books, I chafed at this cloying neediness too, this grasping of Maheshbabu's that insisted I match my rhythm to his tune, never let go of his hand even in sleep. I would awaken on nights physically gasping for breath.

Ila was strong. Whereas my life has been lived as a long lie, always searching for missing alibis, I could never accuse her of an untruth. She was hateful, so hateful. In the five years we all spent together, living in what became a communal dormitory, it was their relationship that spoke the loudest in the house through the night, the chinking of Ila's shakha and pola keeping time to a beat we could not shut out. In such close quarters, oh, we all heard her joyous bangles through the night and had to pretend not to.

Ila had left Maheshbabu for only a few months before she came back from India, but she had lost much of her physical strength. Maybe we had broken her, Maheshbabu and I, but I think her physical weakness was an act to goad me into my worst indiscretion.

She spoke often about the atrocities of the partition that had made two nations from one India. She snivelled, especially about how the changed India had beggared her brothers and killed her parents.

We were all at Mridula's house that day. Mridula was peeling young banana flowers, dipping her fingers delicately in the mustard oil to get rid of the sap. She was seated on the floor, one foot balanced on the boti while the blade curved upwards, slicing the tendrils into minute portions.

I said, "My mother is a minister in Delhi now; the partition brought new opportunities for the patriotic."

Ila stiffened slightly. Then she said, "Perhaps women should attend to their families instead of politics, eh Mridula? So that the daughters don't become the kept women of married men, like common whores?"

I was shocked; it was the first time Ila had voiced such venom. I had not thought her capable of the language she used. Mridula got up quietly and, laying the lethal blade of the boti softly on its side, muttered "Hari Om, Hari Om," and left without looking at us.

I wanted to take that blade and slice as cleanly through Ila's neck as I would through the neck of a scaly carp. She must have understood, for she bent down and, setting the boti upright, she calmly continued to cut the banana flower stems.

I ran to the house next door, where Maheshbabu would be, and bumped into him as he was coming back from attending to Siti. Siti had taken to her bed after seeing the shadow-play between Zainal and Shanti the previous evening, and was still in shock.

"Did you already know about Zainal and Shanti?" Maheshbabu asked me, completely befuddled. "Zainal is unrepentant. He says there is a child, but he will take her as a second wife.

I felt the room spin madly. "A child?" I could barely speak.

Shanti's love had developed over many years, in the hothouse of the times, but I had been so distracted by my own passion for Maheshbabu that I had not known. The way I had failed Shanti could not be spelt out more obscenely.

In that distraught state – my churning emotions compounded by Ila's venom – I dragged Maheshbabu into a bedroom and told him all. Everything Siti and I had sworn to never tell another human being. I shut all the doors and windows, uncaring of what people might think of our need for privacy under a blazing mid-morning sun.

What I didn't count on was Jay, who had crawled under the bed to tighten the screws on an electrical outlet. Jay had stiffened in

*embarrassment when he had heard the door slamming shut,*
*followed by the clicks of the windows, and the sound of his father's*
*voice and mine. He had curled into a ball and shut his eyes tight,*
*while his ears had opened wide.*

*We found him curled into a foetal position, Maheshbabu and I,*
*when the screwdriver clattered from his hands. His breathing was*
*shallow, as if he were holding back an emotion so overwhelming*
*that his lungs would burst from the effort. Maheshbabu and I*
*looked at each other wordlessly and I thought, this boy will tell my*
*Shanti immediately and it will kill her, but Maheshbabu waited for*
*Jay to emerge, dirty and dishevelled, from under the bed and said,*
*"Son, you are old enough to understand why you must never tell*
*anyone what you have just heard," and the boy had nodded and*
*left.*

*It took him four months to exact his revenge. He must have*
*planned it, for he did it on his birthday. Yes, he killed Shanti on his*
*own birthday. When Shanti was dead, Maheshbabu left for*
*America, taking his accursed son and wife. I was left with a baby,*
*Agni, alone.*

*I know Jay will not spare my Agni – he will want to tell her*
*everything, too.*

# Thirty-three

"That was a *great* party!' Agni chattered happily as she and Abhik headed home after saying goodbye to Rohani. "I even got a few *ang pow*s filled with cash."

"I noticed!" Agni could see Abhik's eyes glinting in the darkness.

"I know. At our age, we should be giving them out to children, but the tradition of giving money to the unmarried during festivals is great, and I'm very happy with things as they are."

"Hmm! We need change the *things as they are* but I won't lecture you tonight," Abhik said indulgently. "Drop you home? You'd better get some rest since you volunteered to drive my grandparents to Port Dickson tomorrow morning."

"No problem. I've driven that stretch a zillion times. Tomorrow will be a practice run in being a good Bengali daughter-in-law type."

Abhik's voice was serious as he held her hand, clasping her fingers in his. "I'll hold you to that! But, B, you know they'll take you just as you are. You don't have to try any harder." He drove with their fingers interlocked until the next light forced him to change gears.

"I know. Please be careful tomorrow, Abhik. Your grandfather isn't the only one worried about you. Sometimes, I wonder whether you even think about whether all this stress is worth it... all the late hours, everyone worrying..."

Abhik's profile hardened as he lowered the windscreen to touch the card reader at the tollway. The car glided in silence and they merged into the Damansara Highway.

"You are going the wrong way!"

"No, Agni. I think it's time I showed you what's at stake here, and what's worth fighting for. Sometimes I think you just don't get it."

Abhik brought the car to a halt at a clearing in downtown Kuala Lumpur. The foliage in the square looked lashed by a tornado; flowers lay ripped off their stems and a long hedge lay capitulated, too tired to stand up.

"It took the police more than five hours to clear this street of protestors, Agni." Abhik held her hand, "Here, can you see the streaks? That's from protesters being hit with water cannons laced with chemicals. Helicopters overhead, and tear gas. All this to break up a peaceful demonstration."

"I saw it from my office window, remember?"

He turned to her. "Yes, shielded by the height and air-conditioning. You and I have been too privileged to see this coming. We went to expensive schools, and our money cushioned us from this kind of desperation. You have to see it to believe it. It's a vicious system that keeps people in poverty. Have you even seen an estate school, ever?"

Agni shook her head. She had only her grandmother's word for it. When Nikhil's work took him into estates in remote corners of Selangor and Negri Sembilan, in those early days of their marriage, Shapna would go with him. Sometimes she would teach small classes of children in the estate schools. "Schools," Shapna had said, "they were such a mockery."

Nikhil had been responsible for ensuring that estates had schools but, most frequently, he would come across a classroom, blazing like an oven in the midday heat with an unhappy *kangany*, usually a barely literate labourer, completely ignoring the noisy children. The estate children and their descendants found it hard to escape the life of labour, and today, they were the underclass of this country.

This, too, was her history; an inequity her own grandfather's negligence enabled.

She looked around the defaced walls of the ancient square. Violence became an option when other doors had closed.

"They are really frustrated," Abhik was saying. "No job opportunities in the government or the private sector, and discriminated against when it comes to business licences or places at university." He held her face in his palms. "We have a voice, Agni, you and I. *We* have to use it."

# Saturday

## Thirty-four

Agni glanced at Mridula's reflection in the rearview mirror as she drove through the crowds of revellers. Mridula was concentrating on the road with a slight frown on her face. She, too, was worrying about Abhik.

Not that Abhik's grandparents would ever share their worries with her. For them, Agni was a favourite grandchild, to be petted and indulged, never to be treated as an adult.

Agni felt a wave of love rushing over her as Ranjan's head lolled slightly forward in sleep. He was seated next to her, and a gentle snore escaped from his open mouth. She pushed his forehead back, straightening his hair in the process.

Maybe it was time to tell everyone how she and Abhik felt about each other. It would give everyone so much happiness that her own caution seemed irrelevant. Abhik's grandparents could see they were much more than friends. Earlier today, as Abhik had guided her towards the car, his hand had rested, unselfconsciously intimate, on Agni's behind. Mridula had smiled knowingly as Agni had jerked away, and although they didn't kiss or hug in farewell, Mridula knew.

Not that the signs weren't everywhere. She was acting stupidly secretive, as if she and Abhik were the first ones to be in love in the history of the world, and that only they know the secret code. Rohani had called her out on it too. It was time to tell everyone as soon as Abhik joined her in Port Dickson. There, amongst all the friends and family she had known since birth, so many people who would genuinely wish them well, they should make their relationship public.

Agni felt a burden lifting. The air that streamed through the open windows seemed lighter and fresher than anything she had breathed for a while. She couldn't wish for a better family to marry into. So what if her own blood was impure? Abhik had convict blood running in his veins! The Bengalis had whispered all kinds of things about Agni's father and the *bastard child*, but it didn't make any difference to Abhik or his family.

Agni's own grandfather, she knew, had been a good man who had ended his life as a drunken wastrel. He had believed that they would all return to India one day. Even as Shanti grew sturdier on the soil of Malaya, Nikhil had not wavered. It was part of the family lore, and Agni's own knowledge of the Ramayana was based on her grandfather's pronouncement: *In our Arthasastra, the harshest sentence is exile. The tragedy of Ramayana begins with the exile of Ram; the tragedy of the Mahabharat is that the Pandavas were exiled. Why would I impose this sentence on myself?*

Agni looked at the road opening up before her speeding car, and felt deeply thankful that her grandfather had never succeeded in leaving this wonderful country, as Jay's father had done.

Jay seemed so *disconnected* somehow. She briefly wondered where he was and, with a pang of pity, whether he would have to work all through Deepavali.

Agni needed to re-check the footage of the old man on the video as soon as she got back to work. It was perplexing that Colonel S had denied being at the airport when Rohani had airport security verify that he was a VIP with clearances higher than anyone investigating the footage. Agni didn't like mysteries, and definitely not on the turf that she had to protect.

She felt the tension building up as a gentle thrum on her forehead and tried to breathe deeply.

Mridula leaned forward when she noticed the sleep lidding Ranjan's eyes shut as he fidgeted deeper into his seat. Before she could do anything, Agni spoke up.

"Are you all right, Ranjandadu? Do you need a drink of water or something?"

"I'm fine, child; just a wee bit tired after the party yesterday. Thank you for taking such good care of this old man."

Agni looked away from the road to smile into his eyes. "My *favourite* old man, Ranjandadu. My pleasure."

## Thirty-five

As the bus pulled out from Puduraya, Jay felt like a slice of deli meat released from a moist vacuum pack. In the crowded exodus for the holidays, he had been lucky to get a seat on this dilapidated bus coughing its black fumes intermittently all the way to Port Dickson.

He had taken one look at the crowd in Puduraya, and wanted to turn back. Then, pushed along with the sea of travellers with multiple bags and multiple children, he had gone with the flow towards a bus that was impatiently revving its engine.

It was a last-minute decision to get away from work, and visit Pujobari again. He had asked Colonel S some questions, but received evasive replies that turned increasingly belligerent. Then, unexpectedly, Colonel S had explained that there would be an important military test conducted today, one so secret that even Jay Ghosh would not be invited to be a part of it.

Whether his exclusion from the test conducted today was a punishment for his questions, Jay didn't know. He had given up thinking about all the blogs and allegations, and had left the work behind. Colonel S could keep his secretive military research; Jay did not want any part of this any more. He had practiced, in his own mind, telling his mentor to keep his job in no uncertain terms, but the agitated circles of his finger kept distracting his thoughts.

Besides, no wrongdoing had ever been proved in any court of law. After the trial of the Tibetan Model Murder, only two bodyguards had been apprehended, and they were likely to appeal. Colonel S had not even been detained in custody.

He was tired of being treated like a lowly graduate student again in the presence of an all-powerful mentor. He had done his apprenticeship, dammit, and an institution like Haversham, no less, had hired him. If this kind of a cat-and-mouse game went on, plus the lone secrecy of the work way past midnight, he would just fly back to Boston tomorrow.

An image of a woman, her face shadowed by the lambent tongues of flame from a hundred and eight clay lamps filled his mind.

Maybe he wouldn't go back just yet, but he didn't need this job. He should say goodbye to this job, go to a remote Malaysian island and think about his strategy. He had to keep things in perspective.

He was glad for this break from anyone he knew. He was used to extreme hospitality from Indian hosts wherever in the world he happened to be, if only because the concept of hospitality was so revered in the Indian psyche. But he also found it exhausting. Especially now. When he was with Agni, he felt like the unravelling ball of string a kitten was playing with. But as far as he could tell, she wasn't particularly nice to Abhik either.

A very languorous bus driver steered the way towards the Sungei Besi toll, and stopped behind a snaking line of similarly polluting buses. On the left, a resort built on the ancient tin mines spiralled Moorish columns and domes towards the sky. The mining pool was filled with revellers in swan boats, paddling towards clumps of artificial islands.

A large Chinese family seated behind him distracted Jay with their garbage; discarded Char Siew Pau paper wafers and Tong Garden Roasted Peanut packets overflowed from pink plastic packets. They seemed to have mastered the art of speaking with their mouths completely full, without spilling any of the mush inside. He watched in fascination until a woman extended a peanut packet in his direction.

"Eat, *lah*," she urged congenially.

He realised he must have been staring, but she was genuinely friendly.

"No, thanks," Jay smiled and pointed to his breakfast of *nasi lemak* still packed in white styrofoam.

The woman's head swivelled sharply, and she said something to her companion as the TV on the bus crackled to life. Jay's attention was caught by a familiar name.

"We will follow the activities of the Kumpulan Mujahedeen Malaysia, and examine what motivates this group of militants in Malaysia who have left behind a trail of crimes."

The scene changed to a group of men in long green robes, arranged loosely in a semi-circle. The camera caught their impassive faces, one by one. "Malaysia, long a beacon of stability and peace in the region, has had to come to terms with the problems of rising Islamic radicalism."

Even before the advertisement came on, the programme was drowned by a chorus of Chinese voices, scolding ferociously. They had been passing around a huge bag of sugared cuttlefish, and a little boy and a girl were being smacked for causing some annoyance. Despite the cacophony, a slender young woman on the other side of the aisle remained fast asleep, her *Woman's Weekly* open at an advertisement for fat-burning tablets.

He was jerked awake by the advertisement that blasted *Malaysia, Truly Asia* at a high volume. Surprised that he had fallen asleep so easily, it took him a while to realise that they were at the first stop already.

The Chinese family began to pile into three cars, disgorging rapidly from the bus and waving cheerful goodbyes with loud shouts of "Happy Deepavali!" towards the Indian passengers. The two Chinese children hopped down swiftly from the bus and ran, elbowing each other aggressively.

Jay grinned at the palm trees and coconut fronds waving madly in the stormy breeze, like the long loose hair streaming behind the four little Malay girls who chased each other through the open fields in mad abandon.

It had been decades since he was in the Malaysian countryside, but the touch of the breeze felt like a homecoming, and he felt glad to be back.

# Thirty-six

The long drive to Port Dickson was tiring. Ranjan and Mridula had been fast asleep most of the way. Now that they had reached Pujobari, Agni stretched her aching limbs in the shade of the wide porch.

Even thinking of this building brought the warm glow of childhood memories, layer upon golden layer, the warm and buttery sustenance of her soul. Last year Abhik had stood up at the annual community meeting and said firmly, "This is not just a building; it's a *pilgrimage* for us all," to wild cheering.

Indeed.

Pujobari was divided into four main areas where the community gathered. There was a group of devout fasting ladies who busied themselves at the long temple building; there was the colonial building filled with mythical skeletons in cupboards that the children still ran through screeching; there was the community kitchen designed to hold enormous soot-blackened woks in deep woodstoves that wisely faced the stage so that this area was at the heart of the busiest activities; and finally, there was the bar.

Even at this time in the morning, the bar held a group of mildly drunk raconteurs. The bar had been a part of Pujobari for so long that no one commented on the anomaly of alcohol mixing with Hindu piety any longer. Agni stepped gingerly around the huge bathtub that functioned as the communal kitchen sink, and headed for the barman.

She stopped at the window and winked, "My usual, please!"

The young man on the other side of the window smiled broadly as he poured half the liquid out of a Coca-Cola can into a plastic cup. Then he topped up her can with rum.

She dialled Abhik's number hesitantly, hoping the press conference hadn't started. In her head, she could still hear his frustration earlier. Was it only this morning? *I'm so sorry I can't be there, but this is really important.*

"Hello?"

"Hi, Abhik!"

"Hi, B. What's up?" There was a pause. "Is anything wrong? Where are you?"

"Relax! We're at Pujobari already, reached Port Dickson."

She could hear the grin. "Right. I knew that. How're the grandparents?"

Agni turned sideways to look at Mridula. She was ruling the roost in the middle of a large group of women who were laughing loudly as they caught up on three months' worth of personal histories. The crude trestle tables shook under the load of the large number of vegetables that were being peeled for meals, and the women squatted on the ground, *botis* balanced between expert toes as they cut the peeled vegetables into exact pieces.

"Oh, she's in her element," Agni said.

There was a pause. "I'll drive down as soon as I can, okay? It feels so bloody awful to be away today."

"I know. See you soon, yah?"

Agni held the disconnected phone to her ear and felt the thrum in her forehead get more intense. Abhik was getting to be necessary for her happiness. Without him by her side today, she felt a vague sense of unease, as of things being awry in the universe right now.

## Thirty-seven

*Happy Deepavali! That's what my Agni said to me early this morning, her hair smelling of jasmines and oranges. Then she lit the prayer lamp at the altar, and left for Port Dickson, leaving me alone.*

*I know something terrible is about to happen. I wanted to hold her back, grab her hand as I did so many times when she was a child running into danger, but I could do nothing.*

*My heart pounds in my chest. Today is the day, and she will have to swallow whatever version of the truth Jay tells her.*

*Even when I could speak, I was not able to tell Agni, although this is her truth, this is her history.*

*She has hated me for not letting Shanti marry a Malay man, but I couldn't tell her that it wasn't a simple equation of race and blood. I did not want to lose her like I did Shanti.*

*We tell our children about Saraswati, the Goddess of Learning. In childhood they learn that even if they unwittingly step on a book, a piece of paper, a pencil, anything remotely connected with learning, they must immediately lift the object to their head in a deferential namaskar, for Saraswati does not tolerate any disrespect of her craft. It is she, among all our goddesses, who has no Lord, yet she is elegant on her white swan, and much sought after. Having knowledge in her power means she needs no temple. She is beyond such worldly trivialities. Our children, both sons and daughters, believe in learning. We make them understand that knowledge is the only force that can unshackle them from the tedium of life.*

*Yet there is another story about Saraswati that we do not tell. It is this:*

*Saraswati was born out of the mind of Brahma, the creator of the universe. She was truly his Manas Putri, daughter of his mind. Yet Brahma, seeing his beautiful creation, was consumed by his lust for her.*

*Saraswati, horrified, fled this relationship. But the aged, all-powerful Brahma would not give up. He grew an extra head and then another, and another, until he had five so that she could not escape in any direction. Thus did he corner her and force her to his will. He produced through her mind the four great Vedas, the cornerstones of our religious discourse.*

*But our daughters do not know this. We teach our daughters, through the varnished myth of Saraswati, that celibacy is necessary for knowledge. We make it clear they cannot have music and books and a white swan if they want children too. Choose either one, we offer snidely, knowing full well which way their procreant desires will lead them. We suppress the Saraswati who screams that even our greatest philosophy is born from lust.*

*During the very early days of the Emergency, right after the war, ordinary people feared leaving their homes, especially to travel long distances at night. There was ambush or deadly fire by the communist terrorists, which made an armoured vehicle the only mode of transportation in some areas.*

*Kelantan was one of the most guerilla-infested states, and the government's effort to wipe the black areas white was largely unsuccessful.*

*On a quiet night, in the middle of the dangers of the communist insurgency, a young woman braved the road from Kelantan to Kajang, and stood shivering at Siti's door with a child in her arms. Siti did not know the young woman, but she took pity on her at once. Zainal was away again, on one of his overnight trips.*

*The young woman was gaunt, with haunted eyes. Tendrils of hair had loosened and whipped her face with the fury of the wind. Her features were hidden, then revealed, in the dim shadows cast by* the lightbulb. Siti took in the grimy fingernails that clasped the bundle tightly, the child's hair caked in mud. The child was not a newborn and stirred heavily. The woman looked beseechingly at Siti, making soothing clicking noises with her teeth, rocking back and forth.

"Kak," she said, "Sister, please, I must speak to Zainal."

"I am not lying to you," Siti said with some annoyance. "I do not know when he will return. Sometimes he is in the jungle for days."

Siti looked closely at the young woman. Perhaps a niece from the Trengganu branch of the family… yes, surely, there was a resemblance to someone. Siti opened the door wide and smiled at the woman. Then the woman held out the sleeping child and said, "I must talk to Zainal. Kak, forgive me, this is your husband's child. This is Zainal's daughter."

Later Siti would tell me that she knew something like this was about to happen; she had felt it in the evil wind. Zainal, with his nafsu kuat, so strong his lust for women, and he so handsome, how could she contain him within a marriage? Nafsu, ghairah, goda, so many ways to describe sexual attraction without romantic love in the Malay language, and Zainal, oh, didn't he know them all!

When Zainal had disappeared for two years during the Japanese Occupation of Malaya to work on the Death Railway, Siti had feared exactly this. She asked me, "Can we make something come true by imagining it over and over, Shapna?"

Whenever Siti said to Zainal, "I cannot share you with anyone," Zainal would joke, "Then we get divorced, lah, and men will all line up to marry you again!"

Ah, the Kelantanese and their penchant for divorcees with their earlier sexual experience. Zainal would tease Siti with this sword often. But Siti loved Zainal beyond reason; she wanted only him. When she first suspected him of straying from her, she invoked the ancient tangkal pengasih, a love spell so potent that it would cure him of any love sickness in future.

*Such preparations! Mushroom stones and precious sugar from a jemilang nipah palm, sprinkled with the tears of a mermaid and the essence of the undang palm, to be applied on the body. Siti ate hot chillies and rock salt as she memorised the charm for seven nights from the fourteenth day of the moon.*

*When the spell hardened, became pengeras, she wrote the spell on a piece of paper and drank the burnt ashes with a gulp of water. Thus the spell was in her, to be recited on three consecutive full moon nights. Siti held up her face to the moon, glowing, calling to Zainal's soul Kur wai wait, which would ensure his final surrender. Then the spell passed from mother to daughter, through generations:*

> *I use the charm of love, my love for you*
> *To me*
> *From you, your father's semen is white*
> *Your mother's blood is red*
> *You were in your mother's womb*
> *Nine months and nine days*
> *Born to be a human*
> *Thus, you love me*
> *I use the charm of love*
> *If it is aborted you will die in deprivation*
> *If it succeeds you will enter my body*
> *Kur wai wait Zainal your body*
> *Enter my body*
> *Like a string, like a fruit, your heart's string is*
> *Enter my body*
> *Kur wai wait Zainal*

*Zainal always returned to her. When he returned after two years, alone, even after the Death Railway, Siti became complacent.*

*Then the girl and her child appeared that night, carried along with unwanted debris by the tempestuous wind. Siti became* desperate. I heard the hysteria in her voice over the telephone although she had only said, "Come quickly!"

When I entered her house, Siti hugged me tightly, murmuring, "Why? Why does he do this?" Siti's rage was a vomit of curses mingling with tears.

"Where is she now?" I asked as soon as there was a lull.

Siti wouldn't meet my eyes. "I don't know! Why should I care? She left."

"Where?" I looked around the room quickly.

Siti shrugged. Her gaze was steady, defiant.

"What did you do, Siti?"

"I called Saiful to take care of her. He refused to take the baby."

Saiful, who owed a blood debt to Zainal, and was fiercely loyal to Siti. In the distance I could see the long stretch of mangrove swamps with their thick fleshy leaves; the fiery api-api spread a blanket of orange and yellow flowers, covering the salty waterlogged mud which lay below.

"Zainal must never know," Siti said.

"You are crazy, Siti!"

"Take the child so that Zainal will never know."

I felt a greed growing as the live child stirred in my lap. "Saiful will talk. He will tell Zainal."

"Never!"

"My god, Siti, how will I do this? My husband... He will never..." My voice was a whisper.

"You've tried... you cannot have a child! Take this baby and promise me you will never tell Zainal!"

I made soothing noises. "I promise." Then I was silent, unlike the child in my arms.

Siti's charms always work. She still has her Zainal.

And I? I had a baby to carry through the early morning into a fabled birth.

A fabled baby who would bear the offspring of her father.

Once Nikhil, in his usual miserable phlegm-filled state, had stuttered a Sanskrit verse, invoking the most misogynistic writer of the Vedas: *Na sthri swatantryam arhati*. No woman deserves freedom.

Nikhil turned out to be right about many things.

He didn't live to see Shanti drink so much water that she would not have to breathe any more. Nobody expected the baby in her womb to survive either. When they brought Shanti's lifeless body dripping from the water, and the doctors said that maybe the baby could be saved, it was a small chance, but she was almost full-term by then; my grief dried up. I ran to the only temple, a pagan ruin, to change destiny again.

Maheshbabu brought Jay to me, who, twirling Shanti's pendant in his crazy loopy circles, confessed that he had told only Shanti and no one else. The Sylheti man that she had married by then didn't know anything. I waved Jay away in disgust, knowing that Maheshbabu would take his devil child away to protect me, even as far as America, so that no one would hear of my shame. This would be goodbye.

Then I was chilled by the thought of my loneliness, all those empty years stretching ahead to my old age. I could only despair.

When Shanti's baby became a possibility, I prayed hard. I was frightened by the time I reached the temple, imagining the consequences of the baby growing up, but that was still years away, and the alternative was worse.

The sight of the temple was not reassuring. Battered by the torrential rain, the kumkum stains from earlier prayers ran blood-red on the ground, and pieces of faded red cloth tied around the tree branches slapped wetly in the storm. A decorated idol on a rearing horse, fierce in a way that seemed more malevolent than benign, stared out at the world. Next to the idol, in a hollowed out cave, was the songkok cap of the guardian datuk of the temple, and that is where I went.

It was the merging of the Islamic and Hindu icons that gave this site its potency. Perhaps superstition is a stronger force than any religion in this country, but I had no time to think before I felt the priest touching my shoulder, and mumbling, mumbling, his eyes shot red and his breath reeking of something decomposing, and then the chanting became louder and louder until I fainted.

The will is the only friend of the Self, and the will is the only enemy of the Self, says the Bhagavad Gita. I knew that, for I had willed my daughter's death. But I couldn't, the death of my grandchild. So Agni was carved out of my daughter's dead body, and I created a fable about her mother's death.

And my granddaughter lives. Sweeter than the tree you plant is the fruit it bears. Gacher thekhe phol mishti. My granddaughter lives, and for that I am glad.

## Thirty-eight

Abhik would give anything to be in Port Dickson right now. He looked around the VIP lounge at the airport and indicated to his assistant that they had it set up just right. The leader of Hindsight 2020 was sipping from a cup of hot tea, completely relaxed. He was chatting with a journalist about the parallels between the situation in Malaysia and the African-American civil rights movement in the US as he waited for his turn at the mic.

Abhik's mind was far way. It was his annual religious event, and he should be there with his whole family. Instead, he was waiting for the eminent Minister to start his speech so that they would get their turn soon. After this, Abhik promised himself, he would make the time to go to Bali with Agni.

He checked the monitor again. The Minister loomed large on the screen. He had marked more than two decades as the undisputed leader of Malaysia, and was about to retire. Despite his anti-Semitism and his irascibility, he was the Magician of Malaysia. He could do no wrong and his grandfatherly aspect was marked with the authority of success. His international triumphs had been spectacular, even the seemingly irrational pegging of the Malaysian currency to the American dollar.

Besides, thought Abhik, he liked the old man's liberalism when it came to religion. Too many Malay politicians were belligerent *kris*-wavers, who promised to end dissent with a show of Islamic knives.

The stage was set, and the Minister sat luminescent, the arc lights focused. The press conference started with the gentle buzz of the swarming microphones, and then he spoke. "The decay of Malay culture has resulted in social problems in Malaysia, such as corruption and drug-taking." He paused in between his sentences, looking gravely at the faces surrounding him. He knew the rhetoric well; he had plenty of practice.

"And, although Islam seems to have a greater hold among Malays today, it is merely in terms of appearances rather than substance. Although they have been reminded repeatedly, our culture is still on the decline. In the past, my political party was clean of money politics." There was a pause, timed just right, a gentle shake of a weary head, then the tears in his eyes. "It is not any more now. We explained. I pleaded, I cried, I prayed, I did everything. It didn't change."

Now his voice took on an edge of indignation, as he became the *Datuk*, an irate grandfather speaking to his wayward clan.

"My government is baffled as to why there seem to be more social problems despite the government providing schools with religious teachers. Why does it involve only the Malays? Why not the Chinese? Those with AIDS are Malays; drugs also involve the Malays; rape and murders... Name anything bad, the majority is Malays."

As he held their complete attention, the silence deepened. Then, suddenly, the interview seemed to meander again in its unrehearsed way. "It has become part of the Malay culture. They like it easy. That's why we have a huge number of foreign workers – because we like it easy. When the Chinese and Indians migrated to Malaya, the Malays withdrew. They searched for something easy. If the Chinese had sought independence then, we would have become a country like Singapore. In Singapore, the Malays are the minority." He dropped the singsong intonation and enunciated with emphasis, "When we become the minority, we would lose our status completely."

There was a significant pause.

"It's quite possible that I could drop dead tomorrow." He touched his heart, a subtle reference to his triple bypass surgery a few years ago. "I have been unwell, but never irresponsible.

I did not want to sack anyone, but people do inappropriate things."

He seemed sad as he indicated that his speech was over, leaving the audience to ponder over what was left unsaid. The organisers began to clear the forum for the next speaker. The Hindsight 2020 leader, led by Abhik, walked towards the podium.

They crossed the Minister on his way to the door. The camera panned Abhik, then focused on the Minister, hoping to catch a spontaneous moment that would shed some light on the person behind the legend.

No one paid much attention to the young man in the wheelchair making his way towards them at the same time. The wheelchair cleared the expanse of the room swiftly, and a bodyguard bent down to hear a whispered request. A slight corridor opened to let the wheelchair through. The wheelchair clicked to a stop in front of the Senior Minister.

The Senior Minister turned around and smiled, reaching out his right hand for a brief clasp of fingers before touching his hand ritually to his heart.

The cameras continued to whirr as the explosion ripped through the young man's body with a ferocity that levitated the wheelchair briefly. Then the area was covered by smoke and screaming people and, just before the screen buzzed and distorted, there was the sound of the Minister's voice murmuring, *Oh my God, Oh my God, Oh my God!*

## Thirty-nine

Sitting in a small room on the outskirts of Ampang and watching the broadcast by CNN a half-hour later, Colonel S also called on God, but with gratitude. They played that same footage over and over on all the news channels. The body count so far was six dead, eight critically injured.

The Malaysian Prime Minister's voice shook as he spoke about his shock at the assassination of the Senior Minister. He said this was a terrible time for all Muslim nations, and that it was such a wrong message to send to a moderate Muslim country like Malaysia. The flags were flying half-mast; there would be a national mourning period.

*Moderate Muslim country my arse.* That the bomb had gone off on Deepavali should tell them all something. The original plan was supposed to be two weeks later, but the timing seemed perfect with this Hindu troublemaker coming back on Deepavali for a press conference, and the Chinese now agitating about their dead man at the anti-Graft agency. If the other races decided to fight back, well, bring them on. More reason to exterminate the vermin from this land.

Colonel S glanced down at the building plans, zoning in on one section of a page. The operation had been executed perfectly. The Minister had approached from here; the Hindsight group was placed here... which meant the media had shifted, perfectly, into this corner.

They already had the necessary employee clearances, and had entered through the exit leading to the secondary isolated aircraft parking position. Then the warrior had waited, until it was his time... here.

Colonel S had a brief sensation of unease. Had that Agni been there too? He remembered her swiping her card through the restricted access to the tarmac, and felt his skin crawl in agitation. Would she have been near the stage? She had been so hostile towards him, but also so familiar, as if a mirror had been held up to his memories. Such pretty Malay features, such familiar carriage... It was unimaginable that he could harm anyone with Zainal's blood flowing in her veins.

But the cause was larger than any one person, and he knew that only too well.

Earlier, when he had been watching the Minister being interviewed on television, the noise had come as a background hum to his ears. He had been waiting, a little nauseous from the excitement, and had craned his neck to see the television screen. It showed a large delegation of politicians inside the VIP lounge at the airport, with a golden *kris* gleaming on every doorknob.

All chattering like idiots, he thought, wishing everyone *Selamat Deepavali*, as if the holidays of the Indians and the infidels with their idol-worshipping foolishness should matter.

He had to step away from the television and take in a big gulp of fresh air, and his knees trembled as he sat on the wooden slats that made up the steps to the house. A few more minutes and the Minister would be history. He was so keyed up, he couldn't be still. He wanted to be sure that it would all go smoothly.

Now that the test was successful, they had proved that *it could be done*. The best security systems in the world were useless – and they still had the element of surprise on their side.

The suicide bomber had meant much to Colonel S, but all causes needed sacrifice. He had been their best. It would take time to pull apart the wheelchair and his body. Investigations took time. Their own team worked faster.

Targeting specific leaders could work very well. *To conquer the enemy without going to war was the most desirable way to win*, Sun Tzu. Multiple attacks; leaders must be targeted in different countries. Then attack again amid the chaos. Divert and aim well.

It was not hard to be a step ahead when they had the best brains in the world. When the Devil spread his poison throughout the world, men of science, like him, would rise up to make the antidote. They were everywhere now, and their forces were growing.

The corruption and divisiveness in Malaysian politics made influence easy to buy. Or sell. Their biggest advantage was that they were the most *kiasu* of all the players, the most afraid to lose. For them, the fear of losing was far greater than the fear of death.

# Forty

Running through the open halls of the secured airport, Agni had the feeling of driving down a dark highway in the torrential rain. She felt a force carrying her up, circling her in a steep darkness, slickly speeding on the wet road with a sharp curve ahead. She had to force herself to keep running through her dizziness. The television footage pounded in her head; the soft thrum was now a raging headache.

It was the certainty, even before she had received the call, that Abhik had been there, within range. Agni had frantically called Rohani, driving back like a maniac from Port Dickson, and Rohani would be waiting at the scene. She flashed her identification card like a talisman and kept moving, through the medical personnel, the thronging reporters, the airport police.

When Rohani met her at the scene, she hugged Agni tightly, and stopped her from going any further. Agni could hear the murmur about mangled bodies, dental records, and DNA analysis; it would take some time.

"I *need* to go," Agni said savagely.

Rohani was tearful. "There's nothing you can do. It's like a battlefield in there."

She barged her way in, dragging Rohani with her. She walked past the charred bodies in that grim and silent room. She didn't know what she was looking for until she found it.

There was a body with blue nail polish, just two long blue gashes shimmering with silver, on the toes of a man's right foot.

Agni woke up to green walls, green curtains, a white metal bed, and a blue robe. And a nurse who leaned over to ask, "Feeling better?"

"Dizzy."

The nurse drew the thick curtains. "Sleep, okay? You've been sedated. I'll check on you in a couple of hours."

"I want to go home."

The nurse was young, but there was a matronly concern in her eyes as she lingered and adjusted the blanket. Agni turned deliberately to the wall and closed her eyes. When Rohani came in to clasp her hands in a hard squeeze, her face remained resolutely turned to the window.

Agni said, "I kept pushing him away. He asked me once, you know, *Don't you wish I'd just disappear?*"

Rohani held her tight and patted her hand in awkward strokes. "You didn't know this would happen, Agni."

"I didn't love him enough. I kept pushing him away, not telling my grandmother about him, not telling anyone. Maybe I willed him dead, like my grandmother once willed me alive."

Rohani muffled her voice into her chest and said softly, "That's nonsense, Agni; you don't really believe that."

"No," whimpered Agni. "The women in my family can do this."

She could not stop trembling. Rohani opened the cupboard and drew another blanket around her friend, but it was as if Agni had no control.

**Sunday**

## Forty-one

This is how it ends for my Abhik: two wads of cotton wool stuffed into his nose to keep his lifelessness from spilling out. He lies there still and, through the waving wafts of incense, I think I see him breathing, but then the smoke curls away and his body is rigid. There is so much noise here. The Sanskrit of *The Gita* drones on, as do the visitors' voices and the cries of the women who clasp Mriduladida in grief. All are equally unintelligible. The *Vedic slokas* merge into the bizarre collage of faces until they all seem to be reciting *Om Bhur Bhuvah Svaha*.

I am shocked by the stillness on my grandmother's face. Someone, I don't know who, brought her here. My grandmother is balanced painfully on a wheelchair, but she refuses to lie down, so I hold her. I see in her eyes such mirrored pain; what can I possibly say? I can only rub her back in gentle circles, the way she has soothed me so many times in childhood.

Someone shouts loudly, asking the tentman to create a shade for the visitors. The tin slats squeak on each other and, with my eyes closed, I think of monkeys in deep jungles signalling danger by such high-pitched squeaks. Yet, where is the danger here? Just eyes everywhere, eyes that look into me, into Abhik's parents and his grandparents, waiting for the act to begin.

The *alpona* we had drawn so carefully on the ground, before placing the hundred and eight lamps, is totally smudged. I can't believe I was happy once. I can't believe I was ever happy.

The casket arrives; it will be placed on the pyre. It is taller than the door, so it leans heavily against the gate. Someone shoves a wreath into my hands, and I fumble with it near Abhik's head, overturning the bottle of rose-water. The smell of death and jasmine is overpowering, mingling with sandalwood incense and rosewater. I feel too clumsy for this. I look at the strange covered body and think I see him stirring again in sleep as I have seen him so many times before, on yet another weekend afternoon. Then the fans whir noisily, and the touch of rose-water seeping into my white *sari* tells me where I am.

Someone is shouting for iron keys; must be the colour of nails, make sure; and I stare blankly as they rummage near me. My grandmother's eyes are fixed on a picture of Abhik to be pasted on white art paper. It's a picture I recognise from a dinner two months ago. I know all his pictures, where they were taken, and by whom. We lived the same life.

Then Abhik is lifted up, and he is placed in the casket. His mother is keening, but I can't cry. I see the eyes surrounding us and digging into the depths of her soul. My grandmother's are closed. She claws into my hand.

Abhik's father holds one side of the casket, and I see our friends lifting up the other three corners to the shouts of *Hari Bol* and the noise swells, even as I hear a lady giving another her phone number, "Call me, yah." We are steered towards the hearse; the wails increase. *The Gita* chant is louder through the speakers outside.

Not silence, nor shrieks; I want the whisper of the sleeper's sigh. But, as the coffin passes through the gates, the noise rises to a crescendo, and the sun beats down with the crackle of flames.

Suddenly, Ranjandadu wheels towards me and all necks swivel towards us, eyes alight with anticipation. My head dips to envelope him in a tight hug, and we remain fused in this shared pain that excludes everyone else, until I start to sob. Then Dida lifts her eyes to me, and I gently lead her away.

I will not go to the crematorium to say the final goodbye. For now, I concentrate on holding up my grandmother, who is grimacing with pain. The crowd parts; susurrations follow us like grass snakes, nipping at our heels.

## Forty-two

*My Agni, when she was about twelve, kept a tortoise. She had rescued it from the road and kept it in the bathtub. Now she is like that animal, all curled up and hidden within.*

*She was so closed at the funeral, as if Abhik had been only a friend. It was good Ranjan made her cry, or she would have shattered. If only the world was as simple as a computer problem. My Agni has mastered the blinking screen in front of her, finding problems and solving them, without having to look around.*

*Sweeter than the tree you plant is the fruit it bears. My granddaughter lives, and for that I am glad. I can only chant this mantra in this insanity.*

*When Nikhil brought me to this country as a bride, Malaya was a transit point in our journey in life. Agni has never had the detachment of a foreigner; she always felt the pulse of this country with the insight of a native and, unlike Abhik, she never found it faltering.*

*But we still have too many secrets. Ah, my wild Lute of Fire, I was so weak, I did not know whether to spare you the pain of knowing, or the pain of not knowing.*

*Jay is back again – I saw him circling like a vulture at the funeral. He is waiting for all us all to weaken. He has managed to kill Abhik, I know it, and now he is waiting for me to die so that he can swoop down on Agni and devour her.*

*There are rumours flying everywhere, and the town is a gaggle of hisses and gossipy mouths. It is easy to blame the Malays, or anybody who is not us. Troops have been deployed, just as they were in 1969. The government is saying, "We warned you, this is what happens when the political balance is not maintained and groups that should not be in power get some power to terrorise and de-stabilise."*

There are soldiers on the streets again. They are also human, right? In such times you protect your own. How to blame anyone?

I am old now, a prisoner of this body, and rotting in a wheel-chair, dependent on others. I am the crazy old woman people distractedly pat when they make the dutiful visits that are such a nuisance; such a distraction from their busy, productive lives. I can see it in their eyes as they turn away from me, asking piteously, "It is so hard for you, Dida, so lonely you poor thing," but I know they just want to squeeze out some sentences so that they can go home.

Abhik had never been like that. Our bond was beyond duty, and I knew that he would accept Agni no matter who she was. He didn't need to know who her father was and I saw no need to tell him; but, even if I had, he would have taken Agni, for they were like two parts of the same soul.

My mind is still unclouded and I understand. As well as I understood that day that Siti, wily Siti, who brought my child back from the dead, lost her own soul to a shadow-play on the kitchen wall.

Abhik is dead. I can only worry about my Agni. The vulture circles, relentlessly.

## Forty-three

When Jay saw the footage from the press conference at the airport, he knew at once that Colonel S was behind this.

Jay's bus was parked at a rest stop. Drawn by the hushed crowds around the three television screens, he too had stopped and stared. It didn't take him long, from the CNN commentary, to guess that this was the experiment Colonel S had talked about.

He stared, horrified. Immediately, he wondered how far he had been implicated.

He wondered whether to call someone. Calling his ex-wife, Rina, would be the only possibility, but he would have to wake her from sleep to tell her. He knew Rina; in the current climate in America, she would worry about witch-hunts, maybe even a scandal ending his career. She would tell him, no matter how remote the possibility, he couldn't risk his life's work. *Come home right now.*

He wasn't ready to go back home. Not alone. He could only hope that his past with the old man would roll off his reputation like teflon. He would have to sever that connection immediately and move on.

His mind churned chaotically, searching for an exit route that would allow other possibilities. He hadn't felt such wild stirrings in his blood since he had last been in Malaysia, and then it had been due to an impossible obsession. Now things were possible. Even more so now. Obtainable.

He took a taxi back to Kuala Lumpur, paying double, for the drivers were unwilling to drive into a troubled city with armed guards on the streets. He stood on the narrow pavement outside the huge automatic gates that opened into the long serpentine driveway, and rang the bell three times before anyone responded.

The traffic whistled by too close for comfort, the speed of the cars shaking the bougainvillea plants which cascaded down the wrought-iron fence in white, pink, and a dusky orange before the doors swung reluctantly open. The house felt different. Naturally, he didn't expect to be greeted again by the raucous laughter from a party in progress, but the lugubrious tangibility of bereavement was also unexpected. He had not experienced this in any American funeral he had attended.

Jay looked at Agni from the distance. *How that girl paces! Restless as a caged tiger, and just as uncommunicative.*

He pricked up his ears. In the balmy evening air, he could actually hear tigers growling; it wasn't just his imagination. Was it only yesterday that he had said to Mridula, "Rohani tells me that you can hear tigers from your house?"

Ranjan had answered for her. "Yes, but not because they are still roaming wild! The zoo is down the road from us, and sound travels far, especially at night. You must come for dinner sometime and we can relax and talk, with the tigers as background noise!" Then Ranjan had clasped Jay around the shoulder, "Oho, I keep forgetting... who has the luxury of time any more *bhai*?"

"I'll be back," Jay had assured him.

Jay was back, but now Ranjan was deeply sedated, lost in a sleep that he had no wish to awake from. Mridula sat morose, surrounded by a group of women who seemed to rise and fall like fluttering doves around her. Why doesn't she go to bed? Jay thought irritably. Death was too much of a public spectacle in this country. His parents had subdued funerals, and everyone remained quite composed. He didn't understand this need to call on nonexistent gods throughout the evening in a religious song and dance. People died everywhere. It was sad, yes; even he felt some regret about Abhik, but the living had to move on.

Only very rarely could Death be bent to human will.

When he had been sixteen, so many decades ago, he had learnt this. On his birthday. The birthday he shared with Agni.

Shanti and Jay rowed through the darkness towards a magic shore, shrouded by the inky sky, empty of even a faint sickle moon. Then, turning a sudden corner, they were welcomed by fireflies; thousands of these insects flashing in a transient dance, some stationary, others circling in a sexual exuberance so frenzied that the night glowed with heat. The nightjars and owls added to the soft background chirrups of the night, while tree frogs glided from tree to darkened tree. The *beremban* trees that only flowered at night opened for the bats, and the cup-shaped flowers blew a strong, sour smell into the sudden breeze. Scattered clumps of light softly glowed on the ground as the luminous fungi spread on decaying wood.

Jay's young eyes took in all this in an enchanted glance for the first time, and he fell in love with this land. He wanted to row forever with this magical woman, and this would be where he would one day die.

He had thought of all this in the silence of the night, wondering how to tell her that she was already irreparable, carrying this incestuous load in her womb, but he would make her his own. If he stayed here, he might never become a doctor, but he didn't care. The civil unrest on the streets had been bloody, and his father was urging them on to America. It was time to go before racial discrimination became the price for peace.

But he, Jay, would pay any price to remain here with this woman he loved so much.

On the shore of that black sea, in a place where the fireflies cast no light, Shanti's husband was waiting. That man from Sylhet, the half-educated low-caste *chamar*, how he had begun to sneer at Shanti, his words ringing through the house, castrating them all. This man, who had crossed the oceans as a servant, and could be bought for small change, now touched Shanti whenever he wanted. He could damage her at will.

He had said, "Those people have never been able to treat people of other faiths equally. You were *stupid* to believe one of them would."

Shanti's tears had goaded him on. "Even if what you say is true, things are different here."

"You mean they revised the Holy Book in this country? Hah! I wonder if you have anything in here at all." He had jabbed a vicious finger at her forehead, flinging her head back.

Jay had seen Shanti recoil at that touch, and quivered inside, fearing for what he knew, and the power of that knowledge in the face of such contempt. Shanti had stopped writing, locking up her poems into the same tin trunk that held Shapna's wedding *sari* and Nikhil's silk *dhoti*. The deep cavern which had swallowed Shapna's romantic dreams now drew Shanti into its bosom and Jay could see his love spiralling, unravelling, until she was just a weed, floating further and further in an immense sea.

Jay, half-crazed with the pent-up frustrations of a sixteen year-old, had searched that tin trunk one quiet afternoon and discovered this:

right now I'd like to
write poetry with my nails
on your skin stretched taut
leaving deep imprints
of me; I'd like to
gnaw you till you can't think
your tongue in my mouth...

He had felt a wild stirring in his groin at this celebration of unabashed copulation; that was how it was, the most basic instinct of all, spawning over the earth mongrel breeds... that was the history of civilisation. Then he realised who it had been written by and for whom.

He knew Shanti didn't love her Sylheti husband, but he burnt at the thought of the road ahead. She would never give up this baby swelling up her body so unapologetically; the baby might even bring her closer to the Sylheti. After all, she married him to give the baby a father. Perhaps the baby would be born and sit at this shore, putting mud in her mouth while Shanti told her to stop it, and they would be joined by the man, who would swing the baby up into the air as Shanti clasped his waist, leaning into his back.

Jay couldn't bear the images in his mind.

Love had been a pot, slowly simmering, coming to a boil, and then escaping into steam, evading his grasp. Jay could imagine Shanti falling in love with this man, a man who was not Jay Ghosh, and he couldn't bear it.

Then, on that night while the fireflies danced, and her husband sat on his haunches by the shore thinking Jay was only a child, as immature as the wife he had unwittingly married, Jay declared his love for Shanti.

He knew that if he told Shanti the truth about her incestuous baby, she would die. His father had told him that, and so had Shapna. His words would cause her death, so he carefully weighed his options, still drunk on the beauty of the night.

Which was why he began with a declaration of his love, and only that. It was his birthday; the night was perfect; he couldn't imagine a rejection.

She giggled, unsure how to react. Then she touched her stomach gently, and said, "You don't know what you are saying."

"I know."

She looked into the murky darkness of the water and sighed,

"You are too young for me."

"Only by two years! Your parents have fourteen years between them."

"And they are very unhappy." She shook her head, her black hair blotting the darkness deeper. "Jay, I will forget this conversation; we both will. But I will never stop loving the father of this child."

He drew into the innards of his fury. He knew he had to destroy this love. He said, *"Your love is so unthinkable that Fatherfucker isn't even a word in any of the languages I speak."*

When she rowed him back to shore, telling him she needed to be alone, he had expected her to come back. They sat together at that shore, he and the Sylheti, until the other man hawked his phlegm into the bushes and said that she could go to hell, she was probably fucking some sucker somewhere, she was such a slut. Jay stayed, sleeping off in the humming night, until the commotion woke him up. When they dredged out her body, every bit of her was waterlogged and swollen, except for the demon's teeth.

He looked across at Agni in her white *sari*. Yes, that was what Shanti had become, whitewashed of all colour.

Jay peered at the mansions of the rich surrounding this property. He could find no correlation between his memory and the reality of this new Malaysia. Across the road, the strings of fairylights edging the stalls of hawkers twinkled brightly. With the ambient lighting casting long shadows into the foliage of the huge mansions, this town looked both gawky and beautiful, like a pre-teen playing at being a woman.

He would take Agni away from all this awkwardness at once – this country's terrible growing pains, to his holiday cottage in Port Townsend with its open views of the Strait of Juan de Fuca flanked by the Cascade and Olympic mountain ranges. The white bell-shaped Madrone flowers would be changing to berries now, lighting up the trees with small reddish-orange flames. The green cones of the silver fir would be turning deep purple. He could feel the fresh autumn winds already, and he knew Agni would love that garden. He would take her away from the moist rumblings of every evening, the reek of dankness from an undergrowth fetid with moisture.

He would have to call Colonel S and tell him of his decision. Colonel S would not understand, he anticipated that.

Even Jay didn't understand why Agni had become so important to him in such a short time. He didn't want to analyse this. It was enough to know she would make something whole, something he had been carrying around broken for a long time. And that he could try to make her whole.

Jay felt sixteen again, rehearsing the lines that would change his life. He fingered the demon-teeth pendant. He should begin with that. Approach Agni, and say, *Do you know what this is?* With typical arrogance, she would reply, *No, but I am sure you will tell me.*

Jay looked down at his sleep-creased clothes and smiled in anticipation. He would hand her the demon teeth and say, *This once belonged to your mother.*

Then he would tell her that when a history is buried, it doesn't remain under the earth forever. The muddy river flows, the silt moves, and the past is spit up like *batu lintar,* the teeth of the Thunder Demons – twice as powerful, twice as malevolent.

# Forty-four

It was after five in the evening when Agni awoke after an exhausted sleep. Ranjan and Mridula's bungalow, originally designed for the large retinues of the plantation bosses, bulged at the seams. Children spilled over into the main living room, where they slept on a long bed, tangled limbs in disarray on the floor.

The mourning period would go on for eleven days. Religious *bhajans* would be sung every evening, and vegetarian food served.

People came and went; Agni couldn't figure out family from close friends any more. Her eyes felt gummy with fatigue. Life without Abhik? She had never had to deal with the possibility.

Her dreams were fragmented and confused. She dreamt of water nurturing a translucent baby. She dreamt of nurses who said, *You had tears in your eyes*. She did not want to sleep again.

Even the children were totally subdued. Agni watched a group playing together under the shade of a giant Rain Tree. It was late evening, and the leaves of the tree had already started to fold, but the children played on with fists outstretched: One, two, zom! One fist became a bird, swiftly swallowing the water cupped in the palm of the losing child. The winner didn't shout in triumph, but furrowed his brow and carried on, as if the game was played in deadly earnest.

She touched the flowers that had arrived from Greg, heavy in an oversized rattan basket, bearing the words, *I am so sorry about Abhik. Love, Greg*.

Agni searched the periphery of the crowd for Jay. She hadn't seen him for a long time, but she knew he had come to the funeral.

Her head ached. At the airport, the real threat of terrorism shaped the thoughts of many of the employees dealing with security, beading into the everyday a tinge of panic. Yet, she had not expected the terror to strike so close to home.

She checked her cellphone then put it away. It was stupid to call Rohani about this now, but she hadn't had the time to tell her about Colonel S turning up with Jay. The trail was so unclear that it probably would not warrant an investigation of any kind; everyone knew about Colonel S and his role in the Tibetan woman's murder but, so far, he had managed to stay above the law. Agni would make sure Abhik's murder didn't go unpunished.

She looked at Jay sitting alone. No matter what it took, she would get the truth out of him. Her grandmother's discomfort whenever she saw Jay, his relationship with her mother Shanti, his connection with Colonel S – Jay seemed to be key to the jigsaw puzzle of her life. No matter how repugnant he was, she would have to work on him.

A sudden thought hit her: What if the bomb at the airport was a rehearsal? Only a dry run for a larger, deadlier plot? How much time did she have to gain Jay's trust?

Her thoughts were driving her crazy, and she shook her head to clear it. She would go back to work tomorrow and start with what she could control. She would begin by checking out the Integrated Operations Network thoroughly. Sitting here wouldn't bring Abhik back. Nothing would. They had not made their relationship public when he had been alive, but now, her white widow's *sari* told everyone what had remained unsaid.

Tears pricked her eyes as she remembered Abhik dissecting the national anthem. She heard him singing the lines, *tanah tumpahnya darahku*. This land, too, had a spirit that was thirsty for blood, just like any other nation. Spilt blood was the litmus test of loyalty. She looked at end of her white *sari*, fluttering in the breeze like a surrendering flag. *I have made my sacrifices*.

Abhik had been right. There was so much to be done in this

country. When so many things could go wrong at this juncture, she knew she could not mourn for long. She reminded herself of a procrastinated promise, of being a child of this soil, and of making it her own. *I, too, am a bumiputri.*

There were too many divisions in this land; too much neglect of a shared human history. Perhaps the way to right the wrongs was to start from within. She had to believe that the bombs wouldn't win. She paced silently, chanting an ancient mantra that her grandmother had given her in her childhood:

> May there be peace in heaven
> May there be peace in the sky
> May there be peace on earth
> May there be peace in the water
> May there be peace in all
> *May that peace, real peace, be mine.*

# Author's note

This book had a long gestation period, and I have too many people in too many countries to thank. My deepest gratitude goes to the Man Asian Literary Prize judges who long-listed the unpublished manuscript for the prize in 2009, and to Divya Dubey (Gyaana Books), publisher extraordinaire, for first believing in this book and treating it with so much love and respect. My gratitude also to Anna Sathiah and Julia Gardner, who read very early drafts in Singapore with both encouragement and interest, and to my writing group in Amsterdam (Maria, Kai, Laura, David, Ute, Lisa, Tim... thanks!), as well as Lisa Lau in the UK and Jim Phillips in the US. A significant portion of the first draft was completed while I was at the Centrum Foundation in Washington State as a writer-in-residence from February to March 2003, and I am deeply grateful to the Centrum staff. Preeta Samarasan and Alfian Sa'at provided some valuable insights into the historical-political landscape of Malaysia at the editing stage; Mishi Saran gave valuable editing tips; Mita Kapur gave so generously of her time and the Siyahi expertise that whatever I say in thanks will seem inadequate.

To my Shanghai cheerleaders, Riva Ganguly Das, Trista Baldwin, Tan Zheng, Peoy Leng, Kunal Sinha, and Indira Ravindran; I am so very grateful.

Fellow Malaysian writers who urged me beyond self-censorship to write this story include Bernice Chauly, Amir Muhammad, Kee Thuan Chye, Dain Said, Uthaya Sankar, Chuah Guat Eng, and always, Sharon Bakar.

Details about life in Malaya during the war and emergency years were adapted from: *War and Memory in Malaysia and Singapore* edited by P. Lim Pui Huen and Diana Wong; Andrew Herbert's *Who won the Malayan Emergency?*; and *Netaji Subhas Chandra Bose: A Malaysian Perspective* published by the Netaji

Centre, Kuala Lumpur. The following books shed some light on the complexities of Malaysian society and politics: Goh Cheng Teik's *Malaysia: Beyond Communal Politics;* Richard Clutterbuck's *Conflict and violence in Singapore and Malaysia 1945–1983*; Wazir Jahan Karim' edited work *Emotions of Culture: A Malay Perspective*; *Myths of the Malay ruling class* by Sharifah Maznah Syed Omar; and Mohtar bin H Md Dom's *Malay Superstitions and Beliefs*.

For the historical background of Indians in Malaysia and Singapore, the following works were invaluable: Sinnappah Arasaratnam's *Indians in Malaysia and Singapore;* Rajeswary Ampalavanar's *The Indian Minority and Political Change in Malaya 1945–1957*; Kernial Singh Sandhu's *Indians in Malaya: Some Aspects of their Immigration and Settlement*; Amarjit Kaur's, *North Indians in Malaya: A Study of their Economic, Social and Political Activities, with Special Reference to Selangor, 1870s–1940s*; *Recollections: People and Places,* published by the Oral History Department, Singapore; *Singapore's Little India: Past, Present and Future* by Sharon Siddique & Nirmala Puru Shottam; and Gretchen Liu's *Singapore: A Pictorial History 1819–2000*.

The following poems have been adapted from these sources: "I am utterly enchanted" from Kenneth Rexroth's *Sacramental Acts: Love Poems*; "I use the charm of love, my love for you" from Wazir Jahan Karim's *Emotions of Culture*.

Despite all the research into this book, this is ultimately a work of fiction and does not pretend to be otherwise; as such, it aims for verisimilitude rather than any strict historical accuracy.

## Repeater Books

is dedicated to the creation of a new reality. The landscape
of twenty-first-century arts and letters is faded and inert,
riven by fashionable cynicism, egotistical self-reference and
a nostalgia for the recent past. Repeater intends to add its
voice to those movements that wish to enter history and
assert control over its currents, gathering together scattered
and isolated voices with those who have already called for
an escape from Capitalist Realism. Our desire is to publish in
every sphere and genre, combining vigorous dissent
and a pragmatic willingness to succeed where messianic
abstraction and quiescent co-option have stalled: abstention
is not an option: we are alive and we don't agree.